No Echo

A Novel By

Norm Wise

Eloquent Books

New York, New York

Edited by Elizabeth McLean, winner: the 1999 Tom Fairley editor award.

Cover Design by: www.NoWallsDesign.com.

Eloquent Books
An imprint of AEG Publishing Group
845 Third Avenue, 6th Floor — #6016
New York, NY 10022
www.eloquentbooks.com

ISBN: 978-1-60693-419-7
SKU: 1-60693-419-8

Printed in the United States of America

For You... the reader.

May luck be with you, always.

Chapter 1 — Prologue

MOTHER NATURE must surely have lost control of her senses, not to realize this mid-July afternoon in Los Angeles was fast approaching a hundred degrees.

Automobiles with closed windows, usually provided their occupants the luxury of air-conditioning, as is the case with many driver compartments in trucks and vans. For those traveling in vehicles devoid of this comfort accessory, suffer on.

Garbed in prison togs instead of the expensive attire to which he'd become accustomed, forty-year-old Gino Padonti was on his way to meet a date with a judge…for sentencing.

The heat in back of the Sheriff Department van caused Gino's abundance of fat to generate excessive perspiration, which caused his prison garb to adhered to him like another skin. It itched. This aggravation made him livid with anger at the realization of his predicament.

He was a likeable cuss when brushing up against the patrons who frequented his strip club near the docks. They, however, were the wherewithal through which he'd created his current predicament: charged with trafficking in drugs to expand the Mafia's goals in Los Angeles.

He was accustomed to the feel of silk underwear, shirts and suits against his body; having lived the good life since his days as a youth growing up in the Bronx, a borough of New York City. It was there that he'd become attached to the Mafia.

His assignment to the Los Angeles area some six years ago, involved expansion of the organization's far-reaching drug trade.

He'd arrived with a dream, and enough cash to buy and renovate a warehouse near the docks and turn it into a strip-club of sorts.

1

Known as *'Gino's Place,'* watered-down booze flowed endlessly as hardworking dockworkers and seafaring crews, along with the riff-raff from many walks of life became more inebriated. It was also a haven for prostitutes to do a land-office business.

The two-story building sat on a three acre landfill, protected by a cement seawall that jutted out some three hundred feet beyond the foreshore to the Pacific Ocean.

Located in a rundown section of the waterfront, the area teamed with dock workers and crews from visiting freighters. This fact is what prompted the authorities to realize the area desperately needed such a facility to keep these people entertained in their off hours.

§§§§§

Courtroom 19B was a cool and comfortable place of respite this hot and humid day, and undoubtedly appreciated by the collection of onlookers to the ritualistic judicial sentencing about to take place. However, it was anything but comfortable for the bloodless Mafia henchman Gino Padonti.

Aided by stalwart guards on either side, hobbled and handcuffed, he shuffled into the room's austere atmosphere to stand beside his lawyer to face the judge, when the Clerk of the Court called out: "All rise."

At this point Padonti's interests turned elsewhere. He looked about intently, searching the crowd who'd come to witness the event. Within moments he pursed his lips into a knowing smile that quickly turned into a look of loathing. When he faced the judge on instructions leaked from the side of his lawyer's mouth, the look was altered.

The aged judge who'd recently returned to duty from his sick bed, showed utter contempt as he looked down at the prisoner from his seat on the dais. Subdued chatter in the room prompted the magistrate's gavel to speak with authority. "This court will come to order."

As the room turned silent a grin of satisfaction puffed out his bearded cheeks. In the next moment, however, as though undergoing a sudden pain, he confronted the prisoner with a cold and lengthy intimidating stare that forewarned of a harsh edict. Although sounding somewhat feeble, his wavering voice carried the mark of authority.

"Among numerous other reprehensible crimes brought out in your trial, Mr. Padonti, you have been found guilty of trafficking in drugs. A bane to society that cannot be tolerated."

He continued to look on in a thoughtful pose, elbows resting on the bench, hands clasped beneath his chin while the thumbs ran in circles around each other. His demeanor before he spoke, exuded the impression that his limits of disgust had been reached, and he proclaimed in a stalwart-sounding voice: "You are herewith, sentenced to prison for a term of twelve years."

That said, the air was again shattered like a thunderclap from the sound of his gavel. "This court is adjourned."

Immediately the sentence was passed, Gino Padonti issued the judge a derogatory one-finger salute and spun around to glare at the detectives who'd put him where he was today.

He cried out in broken English: "You sons of bitches—detectives Frye an' Holgate—if it's ah the last thing I do, I'll make ah God damned ah sure, you pay with your lives for what you've ah done t'me."

The guards on either side of the rotund forty-year-old prisoner, turned him forcefully about in the direction of the rear door from which they'd entered the room.

Kicking in protest as they dragged him off, the clatter of ankle chains against the marble flooring was soon obscured, as Padonti cried out in pain like a trapped animal: "An' I'm ah swearin' that on the grave of my mother, you sons of bitches."

§§§§§

Fifty-three-year-old Steve Holgate, senior detective with the Los Angeles Police Department's 32nd precinct, left the courthouse accompanied by thirty-year-old detective Carver Frye, whom he'd been partnered with since Carver joined the force some five years ago.

Holding an honors degree in criminology from U.S.C. in Fresno, Carver was viewed as the cream of the department, due to his diligence at establishing guilt to enable prosecutorial successes in drug related cases.

His ability to ferret out the criminal element in this field had become almost legendary, and therein was a problem. On the ladder of priorities to the Mafia, he'd reached the *'urgent'* category. *'Target number one.'*

On leaving the courthouse, the instant detectives Frye and Holgate reached the sidewalk and walked off to their unmarked nearby cars, the powerful drone of two cranked up Harleys fractured the air.

They came from out of nowhere, and the helmeted tandem riders toting AK-47's, racked up a devastating score on cars parked in the area.

Instant pandemonium took over. People screamed and dropped in droves to the pavement or the cement steps. Some ran for cover behind bushes and trees while crying out in fear, or too alarmed even for that.

A few vehicles went up in flames, and in the next instant they exploded to rain down in pieces on those who'd just come from the court. The area having been turned into a war zone, people hit by the flying debris cried out in pain while police officers lying prone fired their weapons to no avail. The fleeing bikes had gone beyond the reach of their weapons and disappeared.

When relative quiet prevailed, people looked about and got cautiously to their feet.

Amidst a sea of shattered glass alongside a series of parked cars, a man lay writhing and moaning from pain while blood gushed through hands held to his midsection.

Although some people experienced only minor cuts and abrasions from the flying debris, most in the area had come out of the incident physically unscathed, but had the living hell frightened out of them.

It was into this category that detective Steve Holgate found himself as he looked on in abject horror at seeing his partner alongside his car bleeding profusely.

While his heart was doing cartwheels he rushed to Carver's side and used his cell phone to alert headquarters of the situation and call for immediate medical attention.

He removed the time-worn black fedora from his graying head of hair, dropped to his knees and used it to cushion the young detective's head from the glass on the roadway.

Within the next few anxious minutes, which seemed like an eternity to Steve, the wail of police and ambulance sirens in the distance were a welcome sound indeed.

Feeling almost sick to his stomach, his voice saturated with fear and concern at seeing Carver frothing at the mouth, Steve spoke with deep feelings, *"Hold on there partner, help is on the way. I know you're hurt real bad, but please, please hold on Carver."*

Seeing that his partner had gone into shock with blood leaking from his frothing mouth, he said a silent prayer asking the Lord to spare the life of his good friend.

While the seriously injured detective was being placed on a stretcher and also being attended to by medics, in short order he was in the ambulance and on his way to the hospital, four blocks away.

The law officers who'd been on the scene, scurried about to those in the area, looking for any information that might be helpful in hunting down the perpetrators. They came up empty-handed.

This surprise attack was only one of a number of attempts to dispose of detective Carver Frye. Shortly after joining the Los Angeles Police Department as a fully qualified detective at the age of twenty-five, his skills at ferreting out the criminal element had become legendary.

Now at the age of thirty, these prosecutorial successes attributable to his efforts, had rendered him a prime target in the eyes of the Mafia.

Once again he would be on sick leave while recuperating from surgery to his six-foot-two, stalwart body.

While being partnered with Carver for five years, Steve Holgate had come away unscathed when it came to physical damage. But these near death experiences were also taking their toll on him. And they were having a deleterious effect on the force as a whole.

Fear wasn't a benign occurrence to be ignored. It was an attention getter that with each happening, could deepen a state of paranoia and cause one to throw in the towel to remedy their situation.

Chapter 2

DURING this stay in hospital, as usual Carver was visited by many officers and administrative staff from the 32nd precinct.

Margo Sanchez, the Administrator at the precinct, a beauty Carver's age and the one to actually hire Carver five years earlier, was his most frequent visitor. And so it was this time, including her usual kisses on his forehead before leaving his room.

He looked forward to Margo's visits, but being naturally shy when it came to women, he wouldn't let his true feelings for her rise to the surface. Deep down, however, over her many visits he'd hoped that she would give him a kiss on the cheek or better still, on the lips. She never did.

Yet even though his partner Steve had told him that he was sure Margo had her eye on him, and that he should take the initiative, he never did. He simply maintained his unspoken love of her and gone about his business.

In back of his mind while he lay in the hospital, was the grief his mother maintained for a period of years on the death of his father. He'd been a police officer in the small town of Wilmette, off the shores of Lake Michigan on the outskirts of Chicago. He'd been killed by gunfire during a bank robbery.

Even though Carver was secretly in love with the beautiful Administrator, it was this ongoing scenario in his mind about his mother, that caused him to be reticent in making advances to Margo.

On Steve's latest hospital visit with Carver, he found his friend's attitudes toward life in general had changed dramatically. To the point that, this latest attempt on his life would result in him turning away from public service. He'd said that he'd had enough, and was seriously thinking of throwing in the towel.

On this visit, Carver actually began shaking quite noticeably when Steve was about to leave at the request of a nurse.

He'd pleaded while looking up fearfully, "Don't leave me Steve. Please—don't leave me—I'm afraid for my life even while in this hospital."

Holgate was very concerned. He turned back and smiled reassuringly at his friend. "I'll talk to the doctor and have him look in on you, Carver. He can probably give you something that will settle you down."

Carver managed a weak smile. "Okay," he said very softly.

On opening the door to leave, Steve turned back, showed concern and smiled. "Get some rest, partner, and don't forget there's an officer camped outside your door twenty-four hours a day. You're as safe as a church in here." He waved a paw at him, and left the room feeling very concerned.

His partner's state of mind if not altered, could interfere with his job and put others at risk. He would hold off for a time of observation before reporting this to Inspector Charles Dekker, Carver's very good friend in charge of the 32nd precinct.

As was a usual procedure, the doctor's instruction clipboard clamped to the railing at the foot of Carver's bed, was the wherewithal from which male or female nurses were to administer pills or sedatives, make dressing changes to wounds and so on.

The instructions his doctor had written, relating to the wound on Carver's left ankle, called for a *'sterile dressing change every six hours.'* As this time frame worked out to waking him at 4:00 A.M., Carver was made aware of this by his doctor, who also informed his patient that: *'a sterile dressing change calls for the nurse to put on surgical latex gloves, beforehand.'*

Being aware that some nurses were inclined to cut corners and put the patient at risk, his instructions to his patient were: *'If you see a nurse about to change that dressing without putting on sterile gloves, tell that nurse your doctors said for you to tell them to 'F-—K off' or follow the instructions.'*

The time now approaching 1:30 in the morning, a storage room door on the floor where Carver's room was situated opened slowly. First the head appeared, then the whole man stepped out wearing a doctors' smock and a stethoscope about his neck. Clean-shaven and pleasant looking, he carried in one hand a shallow, white porcelain pan covered with a white cloth.

On coming up to the police officer reading a magazine at the door to Carver's room, he smiled briefly. "Good morning, officer, I'm Doctor McLean. I'll be taking a look at detective Frye and see how he's doing. I won't be long."

The officer returned his smile and continued to read his magazine.

The doctor opened the door and went into the room to find the patient wide-awake, bathed in moonlight from a window on which the blind was up.

Carver flicked a switch on the controls beside his bed. The night light on the wall behind his bed came on. "Who are you, and what are you doing here?"

"I'm Doctor McLean, detective Frye. I've come to take a look at that leg of yours." He picked up the information board from the railing at the foot of the bed, perused it for a moment and returned it. "How's the leg feeling?"

"Probably as good as can be expected, I guess."

"Well, let's remove that dressing and take a look to see how it's coming along." He moved aside the light blanket and sheet covering the leg, set the covered pan on the foot of the bed, took something from it and leaned down closer to the leg.

In the next instant, the heel of Carver's right foot caught him flush under the chin, so hard, he flew backwards and struck his skull against a corner of the jutting out bathroom wall.

The police officer came crashing through the door, stopped, flicked on the overhead light and looked about. He saw Doctor McLean lying on the floor, his head at an odd angle and leaking a large quantity of blood.

The early morning news report on radio and TV stations carried story and pictures, as did newspapers later in the day:

'Carver Frye, the much celebrated detective with the L.A.P.D., hospitalized some thirty-six hours ago to undergo surgery to remove a bullet lodged near his spine and to close a gaping wound in his leg, from yesterday afternoon's attempt on his and detective Steve Holgate's life, has survived yet another attempt on his life.

'In the early hours of this morning, a man garbed as a doctor with credentials to show he was Doctor McLean, was killed by Detective Carver Frye. The imposter told the hospital room guard he was there to change the dressing on detective Frye's leg wound, and was allowed into the room. His intent was to inject the detective with a lethal dose of poison.

'The would-be assassin might have been success-ful, had not detective Frye's doctor advised him *beforehand that a sterile dressing change required the person to use sterile gloves.*

Any legitimate doctor, wouldn't have exposed himself to such a glaring error of protocol.'

Monday-June 16

Chapter 3

HAVING quit the Los Angeles Police Department's 32nd precinct at age thirty-one, after six years of service, Carver had gone out on his own under the banner: Frye Securities Inc.

To his mind, this transition from law enforcement to a private practice was a refreshing change. Although out of habit, he still packed a .45 Beretta under his left armpit while dealing with the ongoing security problems of the growing list of manufacturing companies who were his clients.

Having to deal with the many different forms of theft and instigate procedures to deal with this, was a far different challenge than tracking violent gun packing criminals. He hadn't been shot at in the last six years.

The day following his resignation from the 32nd Precinct six years ago, his very good friend and buddy, Inspector Charles Dekker, head honcho at the precinct, had also thrown in the towel to go it on his own in the restaurant business.

A year prior to Dekker quitting, Carver had been best man at his wedding to Helen; a ravishing beauty, twenty years younger than Charles.

The steak house and bar bearing Dekker's name, after being completely refurbished for something like a million dollars as rumor had it, had flourished dramatically.

Just where Charles had acquired that money, along with buying a sumptuous residence in the hills above Malibu, was anybody's guess. Maybe he'd won a lottery or had inherited a bundle. But that wasn't Carver's concern and he'd never ask.

Carver owned a spacious condo on the second floor of a high rise, two blocks from Charles' high end restaurant and bar, known simply as: 'Dekkers.' The premises were under one roof, but had separate, adjoining entrances.

The bar featured a three-piece combo, and an intimate sized dance floor to where many of the dinner trade would gravitate after eating at the restaurant.

Living so close and being a bachelor who didn't like to cook, Carver was the restaurant's best customer. Most of his afternoon and evening meals were eaten there.

It being Sunday, having taken it easy all day snacking and reading, Carver had fallen asleep in his leather lounge chair.

He awoke from a sound sleep at nine thirty, changed to slacks and sports jacket, tucked the .45 Beretta into the holster under his arm as usual, and walked to the restaurant for a late dinner.

§§§§§

"You look well rested Carver, fell asleep in your chair again?," Charles quipped when he entered.

"Yeah, my friend, and I'm starving."

"Right on. Your table is always reserved and ready, so enjoy your dinner."

Carver signed for his meal as usual, said 'good night' to Charles on his way out the door of the extravagantly appointed eatery, and noticed that it had sprinkled a light rain while he'd been having dinner.

He sauntered along a cement walkway through impeccably maintained lawn, took the three steps down to the short, lower walk extension that led to Sunset Blvd.

Rather than cross the boulevard to a shortcut through a treed property to the street where he lived, he figured it would be damp and muddy; so continued on up the boulevard and would cross at the pedestrian light.

While on his way, he found his mind immersed in thinking about Margo, as was happening more frequently these days. *'Was she the woman he would marry? She'd stood out in his mind since as the Administrator of the 32nd Precinct she'd hired him. Wow: that was eleven years ago!'*

The traffic was quite light this evening, and at the light change while his thoughts were still centered on Margo, he stepped onto the blacktop roadway.

While at the center of the four lanes, his mind still in a quandary thinking about her, a black Corvette he'd observed moments earlier on the far side of the Boulevard, was bearing down on him at breakneck speed!

Startled, and caught in its headlights, he was momentarily blinded. In the next instant out of self-preservation, he leapt onto the car's hood. His mind now fully alert to his peril, he grabbed onto the car's wiper well as the vehicle zigzagged crazily on the damp roadway.

The pressure on his hands on the thin metal edge was so intense he considered letting go, but the odd vehicle going in the opposite direction could be his undoing. He persevered.

On looking up he saw that the driver and passenger wore black hoods. In the next instant a gun that was aimed at his head, fired within a nanosecond second of the sashaying car slamming into the protruding wheel of a poorly parked truck.

The car spun instantly about, to head back the way it had come while Carver held painfully to the wiper well. He saw a hole in the windshield above the level of his head, but the guy with the gun was nowhere in sight.

Two angry-looking piercing eyes belonging to the masked driver, saw him to slam on the brakes. The car instantly spun around and Carver was airborne.

He ended up atop an iron grated gutter drain, and although suffering pain he fished the Beretta from its holster and fired, to no avail. The Corvette was beyond range.

After he lay there in the gutter for a few minutes attempting to regain his strength, he sat up on the drain with his thoughts in a quandary, looked up, and seemingly from out of nowhere a young streetwalker appeared.

She knelt down, grinned at him and said while showing more than just legs, "If you hadn't been on such a drunken tare an' didn't stink so bad," she spouted while quickly backing off, "we could do some business, but not tonight, buster."

After she took off up the street, Carver realized that he really did smell. On looking things over, he discovered that the storm drain he'd landed on contained an oversupply of dog poop. And now the stuff was smeared in clumps on his jacket and trousers.

He struggled to his feet, and searched in a trash can further along the street for something he could use to at least remove some of the dung.

Still somewhat in a daze from his bout with death, in the next block he encountered a fellow leaning against a bakery store window and holding a newspaper as if reading it.

He smiled to himself over the guy's charade, smelled trouble, and created his own before the fellow could act. He knocked the newspaper from the guy's hand and said with a disgusted demeanor: *"Even if you had a brain, buster, a peanut shell would make you a Panama hat. Do you have any idea of how stupid you look, pretending to read a newspaper in this light?"*

As the guy went for his piece Carver drove his fist into his gut and lifted his gun from the under arm holster. "Who are you working for, buster? And don't tell me it isn't Gino Padonti. I just this day learned of that creep being released two years early, for good behavior."

"Up yours, Frye, you figure it out. Wow…do you ever stink. If you don't back off I'm gonna be throwing my guts up."

Carver simply grinned, and walked away with the guy's gun.

Chapter 4

SELF-EMPLOYED in the mode of a consultant to numerous large corporations, his time was well spoken for. And to ease the load of a growing clientele, a year ago he'd attracted to Frye Security, Inc. the apple of his eye for years, the Administrator of the 32nd precinct, Margo Sanchez.

In that she and Inspector Mark Conroy, the fellow who'd taken Charles Dekker's place, hadn't seen eye to eye on many things for years, she had quite happily joined his company when asked.

And she's proved to be more than an efficient administrator of his company's burgeoning corporate clientele. Along with being beautiful, she spoke three languages, and had organized her life around a sickly mother who lived with her in an apartment close by.

While at the 32nd precinct, over the years she'd also found time to become a sharpshooter with a .45, had worked out regularly at the gym and held a Black belt in judo.

This was a plus for Carver, in that when he was being pushed from time to time for surveillance on one project or another, Margo quite happily took a break from the mundane to alleviate the problem. Although this could frequently be somewhat dangerous, she looked forward to this respite from sitting in his drab office.

His company was located on the third and top floor of the old, run down, block long Taylor building, a couple of streets over from where Carver lived, off Sunset Boulevard.

The elevators at either end of this sprawling, brick-faced office complex that had seen better days, were a challenge to endure. They creaked and groaned and rattled while going up three or down three floors to the below ground parking.

His always current-year, blood-red Jaguar convertible was parked in the center of two spaces he rented on the third and lowest level. This gave him peace of mind that the Jag wouldn't be subjected to dents from the doors of other cars.

Margo parked in a single space on the floor above, below the ramp to an upper floor.

At the stroke of nine this brilliant morning, Carver opened the office door on which his company name was emblazoned in black on the opaque glass of the door's upper half. Other than the Corporate name, no phone number or hours of business showed. Walk-in business wasn't needed or wanted.

In dealing with his ever expanding corporate clientele, however, some executives had wandering eyes that would get them in trouble from time to time.

Whereupon, he'd been duty bound so to speak, to provide the surveillance factor expertise of his business, as a first step to hopefully alleviate the client's problem. As distasteful and time consuming as this was, fortunately, he was able to pass much of this tedious work on to Margo.

But this intrusion into his normal security business with corporations didn't stop there. Some executives had friends who were major shareholders in their companies, and had developed those same wandering eyes, resulting in domestic problems they wanted out of. On and on it went.

"Morning, Carver," Margo chimed on looking up from her computer when the office door opened. "Goodness, your face is severely scratched. Whatever happened to you?" As he turned from closing the office door she continued. "And look at your hand, it's been cut and you've put iodine on it. Has training lions become a new hobby of yours?"

He remained silent until he reached the knob of his glassed-in office, turned her way and smiled briefly. "Yeah, something like that, Margo. But I'd rather not talk about it, okay."

Aware that an explanation wasn't in the cards, she simply smiled and turned back to her computer.

On entering his office the telephone on his desk rang. He plopped down onto his padded swivel chair, activated the speakerphone, settled back and as usual put his size ten shoes atop the desk's badly-scarred top; its condition on renting here, fully furnished.

"Good morning," he answered, "this is Carver Frye."

In a voice sounding really up tight, the caller got right to it. "Morning, Mr. Frye. My wife has become involved with her tennis instructor. His name is Basil Upton. I was told by a friend who does business with your company, that you take on the odd domestic matter. So I sent you a retainer in the mail a few days ago."

"Well now, this office hasn't received any money from you, that I'm aware of, Mr. Bradley."

Silence prevailed.

Carver smiled inwardly. "I don't ask for a retainer until I know what's involved, sir. And how did I know it was you on the line? Your voice has your name written all over it, Mr. Bradley. I'm sometimes a couch potato, watch the boob tube and find you there accepting accolades for your generosity to some charity."

"But I really did send you a retainer in the mail."

"Well now, that being the case I'd guess that Uncle Sam's homing pigeon has gone astray again. No green stuff' has come through my mail slot, Mr. Bradley, sir."

At this point Margo came into the office and placed a mug of coffee and a check on the desk in front of him. He thanked her with a smile and glanced at the check.

"Mr. Bradley, sir, just this minute my assistant has placed your check in front of me. I'll fit you in, but I really do hate groping about in the maze of matrimony, it usually gets messy."

"When can I see you Mr. Frye?"

"Are things *that* critical?"

"Yes. Yes they are," was the quickened response.

"Well now, I have other matters I chose not to defer, but if things have reached this state, I can be at the address shown on your check at ten this evening. Is that an inconvenient time?"

"No, and thank you. I don't go to bed until after the *'Tonight Show.'"*

Carver hung up, took possession of the mug of coffee and flicked off the phone as Margo said, "The last thing you need is another client, Carver. Oh, and Steve Holgate phoned. During our chat he told me that Gino Padonti has gotten out of prison early, for good behavior."

"Yes, I've been made aware of that, Margo."

"Then you and Steve should grow eyes in back of your heads. I'd be worried if I were you. He swore on his mother's grave to get you both on his release."

He shrugged his shoulders. "Maybe I should stay focused but not worried, Margo."

She came in close, gave him a kiss on the cheek, turned and left his office.

After she closed the door he touched that area and muttered under his breath, "If she only knew?" then sat back and savored the happenstance while chastising himself for not taking the initiative to further what appeared to be—not just a one-sided situation.

His phone rang and again and he flicked on the speakerphone. "Hello."

"And hello to you. It's Sergeant O'Malley here, me buy. Will yuh be comin' along fer yer weekly practice? The reason I'm askin'—we've a new man who's a crack shot, an' I'm wantin' him t'take yuh on."

"Is this another one of your get rich schemes, being the bookie and getting these rookies to bet against me?"

O'Malley laughed. "It's legit, scout's honor."

Chapter 5

ON returning to his office from the shoot-out that had taken less than an hour, he drove with the jag's top up. It wasn't yet noon and his stomach was growling. He'd had nothing in his stomach since last night's Sunday dinner at *Dekker's.*

As his thoughts raced on, some of them involving Margo as usual, he glanced in the rear view mirror and noticed a white Ford van close behind.

Instantly, an unnerving incident was fully alive in his mind as he relived last Saturday's luncheon in the park, with his good friend and one time partner, Steve Holgate. *'The thud of bullets from an AK-47. were again tearing up the grass in front of the park bench on which they sat, and in the next instant the bench was splintered from a smattering of bullets that had come perilously close. Miraculously, both of them were alive.*

His mind's eye again saw them leap behind the bench, onto a bramble bush in back of it. And from this lofty location beside the bush, they witnessed an accident on Wilshire Blvd., the busy street below them. A white Ford van had shot out from a lane between to commercial towers and hit an oncoming car—on and on. It was last Saturday afternoon all—over—again.'

While his heart raced he shook his head to clear his mind and focus on his rear view mirror. He was sure of it— *'that same white van in which two men were chatting and laughing, was following close behind. There was no doubt in his mind, it was the same vehicle, the driver's side front fender was badly dented.'*

Concern for his safety was now paramount. *'Would they be bold enough to open fire, in this heavy traffic?'*

He slowed, to see if they would do likewise.

In doing so, the van pulled into the passing lane, the driver honked his horn to indicate his displeasure, and the guy in the passenger seat gave him the finger.

His concerns momentarily turned inward. *'What the hell—am I becoming paranoid as a consequence of last Saturday's bout with death in the park, and last night's attempt to run me down after dinner at Dekker's?'*

He continued on to the old Taylor Building's underground garage, where he parked in his two-slot accommodation on the third and lowest level.

The place was a *dungeon,* which indeed was what most tenants called it. Many of the fluorescent tubes in the sparsely placed fixtures needed replacing, and maintenance throughout the lengthy three storey building followed a like format, which the tenants had learned to live with.

Rent for office space here, much of which came with its own bathroom and fully furnished, as was his, came cheap. Who in their right mind, if their business didn't really call for it, would opt to spend a king's ransom just to be in a modern high rise building?

The incident of the white Ford van now fading from his thoughts, he parked. Before heading for the close by elevator, he looked intently about while making his way through the dim lighting.

A few minutes before noon when he opened the door to his office, Margo smiled at him and said, "You obviously won the shoot out, or I'd have received a gleeful call from O'Malley, to the contrary, Carver."

"So?"

"So, congratulations again." She got up from behind her desk, and beyond a warm smile she kissed him on the cheek. "That's from my mom, Carver. It seems in your spare time, you had a florist deliver her a get-well bouquet of flowers. That was sweet and thoughtful, and she says to thank you. I just did that for her."

He smiled and touched his cheek where her lips had felt so soft and inviting. "What would happen if I were to send you flowers, Margo?"

"Who knows? Maybe I'd act in a way that would surprise you—and me," she added. Again she favored him with a smile that set his heart aflutter. "But please don't do that until a little more water has gone under the bridge, Carver."

He smiled a show of ivories any African poacher would kill for and looked at his watch. "How about I take us for lunch at *Dekker's.*"

Again the smile. "I'd like that. I enjoyed working at the 32nd Precinct when he was in charge. The two of you have been good friends since you joined the precinct. You were even best man at his wedding, but you know—I've never met his wife."

He shrugged his shoulders from indifference while she cocked her head to one side and frowned. "There's something I've been meaning to ask, even though it's none of my business." She hesitated a moment. "But I'll ask it anyway, why would Charles, a good looking man, fit and handsome as all get out, marry a black woman?"

His eyebrows momentarily lifted. "Love, I suppose," he answered. "She's about twenty years his junior, a tremendous cook, mothers the hell out of me, and I like it."

"Well, you've answered my question, but I'm still left to wonder if love is not many times blind. Anyway, are we taking your new Jaguar to the restaurant or walking?"

"We'll take the Jag. I've got things on my plate that have to do with keeping fit."

"In your hideaway at the Bel Air Sands Hotel?"

"Yes. It's where I can unwind, swim and work out while I'm figuring things that are meaningful to the business."

"I detest riding in this thing," Margo complained as they got into the elevator on the third floor. "I get the feeling that one of these days it'll drop to the bottom with me in it."

As the elevator came to a pulsating stop three floors below ground level, he reached out to block her exit the moment the door opened, and peered out into the dimly-lit area.

When he removed his arm from blocking her, she turned to confront him before moving off. "What are you being so paranoid about, Carver, is there something you're not telling me?"

Before he could respond an elongated shadow was seen moving along a far wall.

He held a finger to his lips. "Sh-h-h, stay where you are, Margo." He reached for the .45 under his arm, and moved off like a cat in the direction of the shadow.

Eyes wide with concern, after a few moments she followed a good distance in back of him in the poor lighting, and lost sight of him in the maze of cement pillars, walls, ramps and vehicles.

Very stealthily Carver closed in on the source of the shadow, to find a man about to climb a metal ladder placed on a wide cement ramp, onto a high-up cement beam.

Before the fellow had taken a first step onto the ladder, he felt the cold steel of Carver's Beretta against his temple.

On turning quickly about, an old man in coveralls croaked indignantly, "Who the *hell* are you, and what in *hell* do you think you're doing?"

Carver was instantly taken aback and lowered the gun.

The old man wearing glasses so thick they looked like the bottom of Coke bottles, screwed his face into a twisted mask, secured his dental plate with his tongue, and after a demeaning smirk he said: "For God's sake, Sonny, put that toy away. What's with you anyway? The name's John

Abigale Strutter, and I'm changing some burned-out tubes. What's it look like I'm doing, to you?"

"Sorry. Some creep has been breaking into cars down here, thought you might be involved."

Old man Strutter came up with a snicker and a delusional shake of his head before he climbed the ladder. He removed a tube and stopped to smell the air before looking down at Carver.

"Some brainless twit on the floor above is parked with his motor running. Here, Sonny, take this tube and hand me one from the carton over there. Soon as I'm finished here," he ranted, "*I'm going up there and tell that ignoramus to shut his goddamned motor off, it's stinking the place up.*"

Carver did his bidding, and the new tube flickered for a fleeting second before turning to full brightness. While looking up for what amounted to a nanosecond, he saw the heads of two men peek over a railing on the floor above.

After his next breath, on hearing a screeching of tires coming from the area, he instinctively leapt over the ramp railing behind him, and landed on the roof of car parked lower down. In the next instant, from behind a cement column he returned a burst of shells at a passenger with an automatic weapon leaning from the open window of the black Corvette racing down the ramp.

It was during this fleeting spasm of time that; from close behind Carver four rapid-fire shots targeted the two men he'd observed at the upper railing. They toppled over it with guns ablaze, to land on the ramp in front of the Corvette an instant before it crashed into a cement pillar and exploded into a spectacular blaze. The car's occupants, and the two shooters from the railing above were being cremated before his eyes.

While reporting the situation to the authorities on his cell phone, Margo appeared on the scene, took hold of his arm and moved him back from the searing heat.

As they stood in awe of what they'd experienced, from out of a cloud of smoke old man Strutter came onto the scene coughing up a storm.

As he faced them in clothes bloodied and torn, he spoke in garbled words from a mouth that had lost its dentures. "You done real good, Sonny. Those slimy bastards will be toast long before the cops an' fire department gets here."

After removing his glasses, and some of the soot from them with dirty fingers, he replaced them to realize he was standing alongside a beautiful woman. "Sorry for the language, lady," he had out after a few more coughs, "sometimes, it gets carried away."

§ § § § §

Within little more than two hours of the police and fire department arriving on the scene, the burned-out skeleton of the Corvette, and four badly-charred bodies had been removed.

The rubble had been quickly cleared away, and all that remained was water-soaked, blackened cement, a musty odor and a collection of vehicles in need of washing.

Being far enough removed from the scene of the explosions, Carver's Jaguar had escaped with little more than a fine coating of dust. But this to his mind called for a visit to a nearby car wash, before heading for their delayed luncheon at *Dekker's.*

It was while they sat in the Jaguar as it was going though the carwash, that Margo showed deep concern over killing the two men who'd been firing in her direction. Undoubtedly their intention was to kill Carver Frye, but they hadn't any idea that a female sharpshooter was in the area, and would take them out in an act of self-preservation.

But now, she was deeply concerned. If what she'd done got into the newspapers, what would her mother think? Her stated concerns grew to the point that, Carver agreed to be the one who had killed them, along with the two in the Corvette. All four of whom had ended up badly charred bodies.

After a kiss on his cheek by way of a *'thank you'* they headed off in a clean jaguar for their late lunch.

On entering the noteworthy restaurant and bar, Charles Dekker greeted them as he attempted to do with everyone.

Beyond a protracted smile at Margo who'd been his Administrator at the 32nd Precinct for many years, he said, "It's too bad you didn't come a few minutes earlier. Helen was in for lunch and she's only just left. She would have loved to meet you, Margo."

"Yes, and I've also wanted to meet your wife for a long time, Mr. Dekker."

"Well, that will come about one day. I've a little time on my hands and can drop by your table to sit and chat if you'd like, Carver."

"Sure Charles. Sorry to have missed Helen, but drop by and chat by all means."

After they'd placed their luncheon orders with the waiter, Charles came by and sat on a padded chair next to Margo.

"We're that close," Carver started off, "you probably heard the explosion at the old Taylor Building."

"An explosion at your building?" The question came with raised eyebrows.

"Yeah, the same two guys in a black Corvette who tried to run me down after my Sunday dinner here, last night. They tried again in our underground parking garage. I took them and two others out, with my Beretta. The Corvette exploded, and they all got toasted along with it."

"The hell you say!" Charles blurted. "After telling me last night that Steve Holgate told you Gino Padonti had been released from prison two years early for good behavior, you leave here after your Sunday dinner, and these guys tried to run you down? Wow—could be that Padonti is behind it. But there *are others,* Carver. Watch your back my friend. That one, is trouble with a capital T."

While listening in, Margo's face showed total surprise before she responded. "It's no wonder you don't sleep well, Carver. You and Steve Holgate have put a lot of criminals behind bars over the years. Goodness."

"And that's a fact," Charles amplified as he sat there looking stunned. "Steve came by here Saturday night, before he got off shift, and told me of you and him being fired on while sitting on a park bench looking down on Wilshire Blvd., near the La Brea tar pits. He still seemed a little shook up, and is out looking for a white Ford van that caused an accident on Wilshire, right after shooting at you guys. He said the Ford shot out from a lane between two buildings. I told him he'd be wasting his time looking for the van at any legit repair shop."

On reading the concern on Margo's face over this latest revelation, Carver figured to change the subject. "So, how is Helen, Charles? Is she going to keep this one to term?"

Another surprised expression lit up Margo's face. "Your wife is pregnant, Mr. Dekker?"

It amused Charles that, even after having worked for him for over eleven years, she persisted in avoiding using his given name. "Yes, Margo. God willing, she'll be able to keep this one. And please, call me Charles. I realize that you and Helen have never met, but one day soon we'll have you two along for dinner at the house. My wife's a fantastic cook."

"Boy or girl?" Margo queried.

"We don't know and don't care. We just hope the baby is healthy. If it's a boy, Helen says we'll name him Carver, after the big lug sitting at the table." He got to his feet and smiled down at them. "Enjoy your lunch, business calls."

On leaving the restaurant, Margo walked back to the office and Carver headed the Jag for the 32nd Precinct parking lot. He ignored the sign restricting use to: **(police vehicles only),** parked there and walked into the precinct aware that his Jag stuck out like a red flag in a sea of bulls.

He returned the waves of those who acknowledged him, and headed for *'Records & Statistics.'*

The bowed head behind the counter looked up briefly when he entered, and dropped down again to continue reading, as though he was on the telephone and simply a voice the other person couldn't see. "Hi, Carver, you know where to look so get to it. I'm pushed for time."

Carver knew Ernie like the back of his hand. It had been his style since the time Carver had first joined the department. He grinned, walked through a door into a restricted area, sat at a computer and punched up a blurb on his new client.

Returning to the counter where Ernie was still involved in whatever, he said, "Your boy Tommy, is a good shortstop, Ernie. I think I'll let him stay on in that position."

The balding head looked up briefly and back down. "Yeah, then he'll like that. How's his hitting?"

"Why not come to the games and see for yourself what goes on, Ernie? All the boys need parental support."

As Carver walked from the room, Ernie's still lowered head talked on. "Yeah, you're right, coach. I'll have to do something about that. Hope our records were of some help to you."

Chapter 6

ON arriving at the Bel Air Sands, Carver approached the desk clerk and smiled.

The clerk reached for a room key, and with a return smile extended it to him. "Hello, Mr. Frye, will you be renewing your yearly lease on the room?"

"You bet I will. Everyone needs a hideout, it's a zoo out there. Just send me a bill in the mail as usual." He waked off to the bank of elevators.

From the wardrobe he maintained here, he changed into slacks and sports Jacket and headed down to sit at the bar.

Randy Grant the bartender, came up to him. "Hello there, Carver, the usual?"

"Sure, but make it a double. I've been through a hell in the last forty-eight hours you don't want to hear about. You left me a message to call you, what's it about?"

After delivering the Scotch-rocks, Randy leaned in close, pointed with thumb and forefinger at the postage-size dance floor and started in. "The curvaceous blond with an ass like a tame bee, is dancing with none other than Bert Mustard."

"Well now, I've only seen pictures of that Silicon Valley high roller with bags of money, which his wife wants a large part of. She's the sister of a friend of mine. But dancing with that chick isn't relevant, Randy. I need more than that to help out a wife he regularly cheats on while living in their Bel Air mansion."

"Yeah, well, I overheard him invite this dish to spend the night on his yacht *Tiddlywinks,* parked at Marina del Rey."

"Yeah, from what his wife tells me, the boat should have been named *Diddlywinks.* But I really hate working on these cases I'm sometimes duty bound to take on."

"Then why do it?"

"Good question. Maybe I like the mix, even though I should say *'No'* to some clients and their close friends." He drained the glass and returned it to the counter.

"Want another one, Carver?"

"No thanks, I'm so beat, I'm going to pass on a visit to the pool and gymnasium. I'll head on back to my room, and crash until it's time for me to leave for a ten o'clock appointment."

Chapter 7

CARVER didn't have to wonder about the location of Mr. Bradley's home in the hills above Malibu. He knew Rushton Place road was adjacent to a small park at the top of a knoll, little more than a stone's throw from where his good friends Charles and Helen Dekker lived on Peacock Crescent.

He turned from the freeway onto the exit that would take him into the Malibu Hills, and slowed to a leisurely pace to enjoy the serenity. This was heaven, compared to the madhouse of screeching tires, honking horns, foul-mouthed threats and innovative responses he'd left behind,

At the touch of a button he opened up the top, fully able to appreciate the music from the stereo mixing with the gentle breezes invading the car's cockpit.

But the peacefulness wasn't to last. The wail of sirens coming ever closer caused him to pull to a side of the road. A black-and-white and an unmarked car with roof lights flashing, were hightailing it up the hill.

On reaching the hill's uppermost road, he glanced at the dash to learn it was within a few minutes of his appointment.

On Rushton Place Road he rounded a sharp curve and began the search for Bradley's address.

There were no street lamps in the area. Only the eerie glow from decorative lamps hidden low in stonework walls, or from elaborately designed lamps atop them.

Electronically operated wrought iron gates abounded, a precursor to let one know this is protected territory. Its residents didn't want your visit, your business, or your finger on the mother-of-pearl call button to ask questions of the butler, or whomever, unless you were expected.

But this protocol had been circumvented at the Bradley address, illuminated on a polished brass plate recessed in the niche of a stone-faced gate post.

The gate being wide open, he entered a long drive of interlocking red bricks, so heavily treed on both sides the overreaching branches created a sparsely lit tunnel. Wherein, the infrequently spaced curb lighting created an eerie glow.

At its far end, a sharp turn exposed a wide expanse of openness within a parameter wall of sculpted emerald green firs. At the center of this large, bricked-surfaced parking area, stood a magnificently lit four-tiered fountain, where the veil of water slipping from level to level appeared like liquid silver.

Nosed into a manicured hedge of bougainvillea, fronting the mansion at this low level, a kaleidoscope of color from the flashing police car lights, looked as out of place as a tree in a desert.

At the crest of a beautifully landscaped gradual rise, some twenty feet higher than the fountain level, was a spectacular mansion of Spanish influence that must have cost many millions.

Carver was impressed. He'd visited the residences of a few celebrities, business tycoons and the like, but nothing as grandiose as this.

Apart from a wide expanse of cliff area that offered an uninhibited view of the Pacific and its sunsets, the remainder of the large cliff-top property was delimited by a high, stone-faced cement wall. Atop which, was a layer of what appeared to be glass fragments that glistened like diamonds from subdued lighting placed along its crest.

The grounds he could see from the lighting placed at random, showed that the spacious property contained a profusion of emerald-green lawns, towering palms, flowering shrubs and evergreens sculpted into a variety of shapes. Waterfalls flowed into ponds resplendent with water lilies, and magnificent marble statues stood about like sentinels on watch.

He was certain there was much that he'd missed, but he did notice a tennis court and a pool area, while he climbed the wide sections of stairs that diminished in width on reaching a people-gathering plateau at the mansion's spectacular entranceway.

This area was lit by torch-shaped lamps on either side of the enclosed archway; protection from the elements for the elaborately carved entrance doors within.

Upon using the metal knocker, one of the massive doors opened, and Carver was met by the silent stares of a young, officially garbed police officer who broke into an amused grin.

"Hot damn," the officer spouted. "Detective Holgate was just talking about you before we left the station, and here you are as large as life."

Carver grinned inwardly. "Is Steve Holgate here?"

"Yes, along with his partner. Come along with me, detective Frye. I'll take you to him. By the way, I'm Officer Rod Strudwick."

He followed the officer into a cavernous, marble-clad entrance hall, past a magnificently crafted cornucopia staircase leading to an upper landing. The officer stopped suddenly, took in the whole room with a sweep of his arm and said quietly, as though revealing a secret, "Really somethin,' huh?"

Through a wide archway they entered the elegantly furnished living area, the most dominant feature being a massive floor-to-ceiling fireplace. "He's over there," the officer said and pointed.

Carver walked off towards the center of a high-ceilinged room, where Steve Holgate was talking to someone seated on a couch.

He held out his hand and they shook, as a look of dismay clouded Steve's face. "What brings you here, Carver? You tapped into our police calls looking for business?"

Carver answered with a smile that was more a grin, and glanced down at a beautiful young woman employing a handkerchief to her tearful eyes. Her torn dress adequately disclosed breasts so ergonomically suited to the rest of her, it was obvious the Good Lord had worked overtime to achieve such perfection.

The beauty of her face was marred with tears, and they, along with blood dripping from a couple of minor lacerations on her forehead, had smeared her makeup. Her long, blond hair was disheveled and matted with blood.

He glanced at Steve and moved his head slightly in the direction of the woman. "Mrs. Bradley?" he queried softly.

On receiving a confirming nod, Carver disclosed that he had a ten o'clock appointment with Mr. Bradley. "Is he somehow involved here" he continued, nodding to indicate the weeping woman seated on the white silk fabric of an overstuffed settee.

"According to Mrs. Bradley, he is. And not just for what you see here. Mrs. Bradley's sister, Beverly Hughes, is with a new intern recently assigned to me, named James Hickey. They are in the family room along the hall. Miss Hughes is giving her side of what happened here. She was also attacked."

He stopped for breath for a few seconds and continued.

"Apparently, Morton Bradley had been drinking heavily in his second floor study after dinner. And according to Mrs. Bradley, drunk as a coot he appeared in the living room where the two women were chatting. He accused his wife of infidelity, grabbed the front of her dress and lifted her bodily to her feet from where she was sitting alongside her sister. When he started slapping her around, the sister attempted to interfere but was left bleeding and unconscious on the floor."

"Have you spoken with Mr. Bradley?"

"No, we've pounded repeatedly on his locked study door, with no response. He's probably passed out in there. The door is a rustic slap of solid oak, supported by three massive wrought iron hinges that extend almost the width of the door. Our shoulders couldn't budge it, even a fraction of an inch."

"Doesn't the staff have a key to his study?"

"Not according to Mrs. Bradley. That room is his private domain. Only the housekeeper is allowed to clean and dust from time to time when he's there. It's her day off, along with the maid's and the cook's. Only the butler is around, a fellow of maybe seventy. He's been with Mr. Bradley for years, according to Mrs. Bradley."

"Try and rest, Mrs. Bradley," Steve said compassionately, in hopes of stopping the woman's sobbing, "we've phoned for your doctor, he should be along soon."

He turned back to Carver. "Bradley must have passed out from too much booze. Maybe now he's returned to the land of the living, but don't count on him keeping your appointment. From the job he's done on the sisters, he'll be under arrest for assault." He turned to walk off.

"Mind if I tag along?"

"Suit yourself, Carver."

They left the room and entered a long hallway, where Steve poked his head through an open doorway and spoke to his partner. "This is detective Carver Frye, Hickey. He and I are off to the study, how are you making out here?"

The fledgling detective and Carver, having met in the shootout earlier in the day, simply acknowledged one another with smiles.

James Hickey was three inches over six feet, his skin was the color of skim milk, and that allowed the veins in his forehead to show through. Along with having a mop of thinning blond hair, his overbite would put a donkey to shame.

He brought Steve up to date on what Beverly Hughes had been telling him of the incident.

"That's exactly what happened, officer," a traumatized Miss Hughes said, on taking a towel smeared with blood from her face.

Steve's expression disclosed that he figured as much.

Carver smiled briefly at the beautiful brunette who, but for the color of her hair, bore a striking resemblance to her sister.

"Well," Steve continued, speaking to the fledgling detective, "some time ago, I sent officer Strudwick's partner, Len Watson, to search out the butler in the hope he knows where there's a ladder long enough to reach the study balcony. Check it out, Hickey. And now that you've taken Miss Hughes' statement, you can escort her back into the living room. The sisters might want to comfort one another, now that things are back on track with nothing more to fear from their attacker. Carver and I are going upstairs to the study."

Before they'd taken two steps along the hallway, officer Len Watson appeared, saw Carver whom he knew well, and said, "Well now—reinforcements from the private sector? Hello, Carver. What in hell are *you* doing here?"

Steve looked at the officer in a manner that told him to shut up without him saying so. Officer Watson realized he'd stepped out of bounds and started to explain.

"It took me fifteen minutes to find that old buzzard the butler. I found him in the wine cellar, and he was..."

"Hold it," Steve interjected, moving his hands back and forth in front of the officer's face, "I'm not looking for a running account of your exploits. Answer the question. Did you locate a ladder for us?"

"Yes sir, it's put up and resting against the top railing of what the butler says, is the balcony of Mr. Bradley's study."

"First rate, officer Watson. See that the doctor is let in when he comes to attend to Mrs. Bradley and her sister."

At the end of a long second floor hallway, hung with what appeared to be art from the likes of Goya and Picasso, Carver had the feeling that he'd just paid a quick visit to an art gallery. They now faced the imposing Spanish type door that Steve had described earlier.

While Steve hammered on it with his fists, Carver noticed what looked like blood seeping onto the hallway carpet from under the door. "Take a look," he said pointing, as Steve was about to clobber the door with the butt of his service revolver.

A look to where Carver had pointed, caused Steve to turn to his friend with a confirming nod. "Looks like blood to me."

In the next moment they were walking the balustrade hallway Carver had noticed at the top of the cornucopia staircase, which led to the marble-clad entry below.

Before reaching the top of the stairs, they observed officer Strudwick talking with a distinguished looking fellow who resembled Steve Holgate in physical stature, and was also wearing clothing somewhat similar. A dark suit clung to his hefty frame, and he also wore a wide-brimmed, black fedora.

The officer's voice resonated clearly in the high ceiling of the entryway. "I'm sorry, sir, but I can't allow you to go upstairs, unless it's cleared by detective Holgate."

"Are you Mrs. Bradley's doctor?" Steve called down from the top of the stairs.

"No," the stranger said on looking up, "my name is Victor Spencer. I am Mr. Bradley's business partner and have just this morning returned from a six-month holiday in Europe. We are old friends and usually watch the Tonight Show together. We talked on the phone this morning. He's expecting me." A confused look now clouded his countenance and he said in the next breath, "What, may I ask, are the police doing here? Is Mr. Bradley, all right?"

"We are not sure about anything at the moment, Mr. Spencer. Please let the officer escort you into the living room. He will want a complete record of whom you've been with since your arrival this morning. Times and whatnot, I expect will be of help too."

"But I..."

"Come along with me, Sir," officer Strudwick said and took Mr. Spencer by the arm as the detectives started down the staircase.

The night was cool, and under a full moon, low clouds coming inland from the Pacific turned the area into a constantly changing patchwork quilt. Now closing in on eleven o'clock, Steve Holgate and Carver met detective Hickey at the base of the ladder. Hickey was the first to climb in the relative darkness, and Steve went up next.

No lighting had been planned for in this area of the mansion, as it would detract from the spectacular view of the ocean and its sunsets. There were, however, unlit torch-like fixtures attached to the decorative stonework walls on either side of the spacious balcony, and above a wall of glass with a sliding door.

Intermittent splashes of moonlight illuminated a large balcony, enclosed by a decorative, three-foot-high parapet wall.

Before Carver began to climb the ladder, he moved aside the heavy foliage of ivy that had been growing up the decorative stone-faced walls for years, in this and other areas of the mansion. Tightly matted, he noted that it clung securely to a sturdily-built wooden trellis which, over the years the ivy had completely obliterated from view.

Taken aback with surprise on parting the foliage, he'd exposed what looked like fresh scuffmarks on a horizontal section of the hidden trellis. They appeared to have been made by shoes. He looked closer.

"What's taking you so long to get up here, Carver?" came the irate voice of his one-time partner from beyond the above railing.

"I'll get there when I get there," Carver called out, bemused that even after six years, Steve couldn't let go of the fact he'd gone out on his own.

While climbing the ladder just barely long enough to reach the balcony railing, which resulted in it being close to the ivy-covered wall, Carver took a penlight from his pocket and reached out to find what appeared to be more shoe abrasions on the hidden trellis beneath the ivy.

He returned the penlight to his pocket and dropped onto the balcony decking to observe the detectives contemplating a locked sliding glass door.

"The drapes are closed up so tight, we can't even get a peep inside," Steve grumbled on confronting Hickey; "so how do we get in to learn who's leaking that blood onto the carpeted hallway floor?"

The intern detective grinned and shrugged his shoulders. "Maybe call a locksmith?"

"The lock is on the inside of that door, Hickey. But you're right—we do call a locksmith." He reached for his service revolver, bashed at the glass, and kept at it until there was a lengthy opening large enough for a person to ease through and open wide what appeared to be heavy drapes and the locked, sliding glass door.

Aware that he was the matchstick in the group, without any preamble Hickey eased his way very carefully past treacherous looking shards of glass just waiting for him to make a mistake.

After a breathtaking minute, he reached the wall of heavily lined drapes, dropped to his knees and made his way under them into the room.

While the seasoned detectives stood waiting for the door's locking latch and drapes to be opened up, they heard detective Hickey cry out: *"Holy Mother of God."*

During their next few breaths, after bashing out a little more glass, considerably more; Steve and Carver were through the door, and fought their way through the heavy drapes into a room that was brilliantly lit.

Hickey was standing as though frozen in time, while looking down at the body of a man who lay slumped against the base of the upper hallway study door.

The eyes of the corpse were wide open, and a pain-filled expression was etched into a bloodless face smeared with gore. Morton Bradley lay in a pool of his blood that had drenched his white shirtfront, and run down to the crotch of his trousers to form a pool, spread about by hand and leg movements during the last throws of his life. It was a gory, sickening site to behold, even for the veteran detectives.

Carver had seen all manner of killings during his tenure with the Los Angeles Police Department, but rarely anything as pitiful as this. The lifeless eyes staring up at him, held in them the dying man's clamor for help while his blood-soaked hands gripped the steel shaft of a deeply embedded arrow in his chest.

He reached out and closed the dead man's eyes, took Hickey by the arm to sit him down on a chair, in what on first glance was a spacious and very expensively furnished study.

As Steve looked about, he used his cell phone to inform headquarters of the situation, while Carver located the cord that would open up the drapes, aware that a contingent of forensic specialists would be arriving on the scene within the hour.

Meanwhile, as though still connected to the force, he worked alongside Steve.

Having regained a hold on life, Hickey was now seated at the dead man's desk set back and facing the safe, to record everything Steve was taking from the opened safe, along with whatever else Carver found on the floor alongside the desk front.

This was the young detective's first exposure to such a gruesome scene, and as time went on he would have to learn to cope with the mind sapping stress that frequently came with the profession, or bow out.

It was established that the sliding glass door to the balcony, and the study door off the upper hallway, had both been locked, and bolted at the bottom on the inside. This gave caused for the detectives to believe that Bradley had become paranoid about his safety for some reason. The two seasoned detectives looked at one another, completely bewildered.

"How does one get shot by an arrow in a locked and bolted shut room?" Carver remarked, hands tucked under his arm pits in a thoughtful pose. "The only thing open is a safe that was undoubtedly installed along with the fireplace, during the mansion's construction in what I'd guess is a cement wall four feet thick in this area. The safe and fireplace also have a decorative inner wall of red bricks, where the safe hides behind a hinged-closed painting, by Picasso."

While their observations continued, Carver flicked a switch to light the torch lamps on the balcony. They returned outside through the now fully opened sliding door with the broken glass.

The area now well illuminated, they saw that the outside wall here, as with much of the mansion's exterior elsewhere, was an off-white cement in which a decorative display of random sized cut stones were implanted to replicate the antiquity one sees in castles throughout Europe.

While they awaited the arrival of a forensic team of experts, they seemingly appeared in wonder of it all, as a detailed listing of the safe's contents went on by fledgling detective James Hickey, seated at the slaughtered man's desk.

After Hickey had recorded the various contracts and detailed the loans made to various individuals and company's; he recorded the sizeable quantity of large denomination paper money. He then set about recording the pieces of jewelry from the safe. It looked expensive, and the fledgling detective had been well versed during his training, on how to give a detailed description and estimated value.

Chapter 8

IT was 1:00 A.M. Tuesday morning when the coroner, the print men and forensic specialists left the murder scene. The corpse having been placed on a gurney with the steel arrow left sticking up from its chest, made a tent of the sheet covering the body being wheeled away.

In the mansion's marble-clad foyer, detective Holgate was informed by Officer Watson, that the sisters had been given sedatives by their doctor. "He left about an hour ago, and said they'd be out for the night," the officer elaborated.

"Is there anything else, Len?"

"Yeah, the household staff returned shortly after midnight, and I phoned for a carpenter to nail some sturdy plywood over the sliding balcony door with the broken glass."

"Good work. You and your partner stick around until the carpenter is finished, and make sure that balcony door is securely locked top and bottom, as we originally found it. Make sure you lock the study door when you leave with the key taken from the vest pocket of the deceased, and seal it with: *'Do Not Enter'* tape, declaring it a *'crime scene'.*"

He turned back to Carver and they walked from the mansion to beyond the brief archway at the mansion's entrance, where they stood talking in the open gathering area lit by torch lamps on either side of the archways outer wall.

Before heading down the series of stairs and landings to the fountain and parking area, detective Holgate remarked in all sincerity, "Thanks for your help tonight Carver, but I'm afraid this case will make it into the unsolved files."

"You could be right, Steve. That study and safe was gone over with a fine-toothed comb by you and me, along with numerous other trained people until hell wouldn't have it."

"Yeah, it's a mystery all right, Carver," he agreed. And while wearing a questioning look he said: "In going through Bradley's personal checkbook, I see he'd written you one for ten thousand dollars just a few days ago. What's that all about?"

Carver grinned. "That's a private matter."

Steve returned the grin. "The way the mails are these days, you probably haven't received it. I can put in a stop payment order, you know. Ten grand covers a lot of investigating, and I sure could use your help on this case, wudduysay?"

Carver's grin continued. "The check's been certified and deposited to my business account."

"Okay—you've got me. Anyway, it's just past one on a Tuesday morning, June 17th—the starting time by your credo that, if a case isn't solved within seventy-two hours, its likelihood of being solved is slim indeed."

"I said that?"

"Yeah. So if you're game, smarty, even with you helping out on this mystery, I'll bet a hundred that your time frame will go by the boards and this case ends up in the unsolved files."

A look of serious interest was captured on Carver's face. "You may be right on this one, Steve. So, forget the bet. Wild horses couldn't keep me from this one. And to keep you informed good buddy, the reason I'm here is to secure evidence on Bradley's wife, whom he suspected was having an affair."

"That bears looking into," Steve remarked as Victor Spencer emerged onto the open decking gathering area, rubbing his eyes awake while struggling into his suit jacket. He came up to Steve wearing a mask of concern and his ever-present hat.

"I fell asleep in the den while biding my time waiting to talk with you, detective Holgate. Seems I've caught up to you just in time. You look about ready to leave. I wanted to ask when the important documents from my partner's safe will be released to me."

"Not until I'm finished with them, Mr. Spencer, and I can't tell you right now, when that will be."

Steve and Carver moved off a step towards the stairs to the parking area and Spencer followed. He touched Steve Holgate on the arm to gain his attention, intent on changing the detective's mind, and continued to argue while they stood there exchanging words.

Now almost one-thirty in the morning, the moon hidden behind a thick layer of cloud, they'd have been in total darkness were it not for the simulated torch lighting on either side of the arched entrance enclosure.

The instant Steve turned from Victor Spencer to join Carver and head on down the stairs; the unmistakable crack of a rifle shot split the night air.

Steve dropped like a stone onto the tiled decking as blood spurted through a hole in his suit jacket in the area of his heart.

Carver's immediate fear was that the next shot would be for him, that Gino Padonti was making good on his threat to kill them both on being released from prison. In the next instant he was kneeling at Steve's side and dialing his cell phone for help, while looking onto a face etched in pain. Another shot rang out. His phone was nicked by a bullet and went flying. His Beretta instantly appeared from its holster and coincidental with knocking Victor Spencer to the decking as he stood there in shock, he fired at the torch lights.

They were now in total darkness.

On removing Steve's hat to place it under his head, he saw that he'd gone into shock, was frothing at the mouth and that his breathing was shallow as he looked up at Carver in fear, his eyes the size of saucers.

As Carver prayed to God, asking Him to spare his friend's life, he removed his jacket and placed it over his friend to keep him warm.

Detective James Hickey and the two uniformed police officers came running onto the scene, and froze in their tracks as they looked on.

"For God's sake James, phone for an air ambulance!" Carver barked. "And you fellows, get up to that outcropping on the hillside where the shots came from. I want that shooter *real bad.*"

After what seemed an eternity, but in reality a few minutes, a chopper appeared overhead. Carver said a prayer of thanks to the Lord as it quickly lit its way onto the parking area, bathed in the light from the fountain.

Along with the staccato sounds of the chopper's blades fracturing the night air, and noise from the arriving police vehicles equipped with sirens and barking dogs, the multiplicity of sounds was almost ear splitting.

Four police cruisers arrived over the space of some three minutes, to disgorged eight more officers and two police dogs, while the medics from the chopper immediately attended to the needs of detective Holgate.

Strapped onto a stretcher for the flight to the hospital, Steve was hurried down the stairs to the chopper.

Meanwhile, Carver had alerted the officers who'd arrived as to what had happened, and had them searching for the shooter with powerful flashlights and barking dogs.

Within minutes another chopper was overhead, flooding the area with its intense beam of light to aid in capturing the sniper.

As Carver stood there in the darkness asking God to spare the life of his friend, James Hickey placed an arm about his shoulders in a show of compassion.

Carver smiled warmly at him. "Get some shuteye, James, and don't forget to stay in touch to keep me informed. I promised Steve that I'd get my teeth into this case, and I don't have time to waste."

Tuesday-June 17

Chapter 9

IT was closing in on two in the morning, when Carver got in behind the wheel of his convertible and sped from the mansion parking area.

The freeway at this hour was civilized, and he put his foot to the floor on his way to the dock area, where Gino Padonti hung out on the top floor of a two-story strip joint he owned, known as *'Gino's Place.'* His office was at the top of the stairs to the left of the landing, his living quarters to the right.

The clientele were mostly dope addicts, peddlers, lonely seamen, pimps, hustlers and whores. On occasion when he was on tap with the L.A.P.D., he and Steve would find the occasional blue blood slumming there.

A blinking light on his dash cautioned that he was low on fuel, nature called to say he should empty his bladder, so he pulled in at a gas bar a block from Gino's Place to act on priorities, when his cell phone played its programmed tune.

On flipping it open, he learned that Charles Dekker's replacement, Inspector Mark Conroy, was on the line. "Yes—Inspector Conroy?" he said testily.

"Knowing that you and Steve Holgate are the best of friends, Carver, I wanted to touch base with you about his condition. It's critical, but the surgeon I spoke with only moments ago, gives him a 50/50 chance for a full recovery."

The inspector kept on talking, but his words were simply background mumbo-jumbo until Carver had finished his prayer asking God to spare Steve's life.

"——————————————and now that Gino Padonti's been released, be extra cautious or you could be next, Carver."

His statement carried an element of conjecture that twigged Carver's curiosity. "You're saying for sure, that Padonti is the culprit here?"

"That's not for certain, but it's a definite probability. The department is so understaffed and loaded down with cases at this time, I was hoping you would work with us on this."

Carver was silent a moment.

"Will you at least consider it? We have to pull out all stops when one of our own is taken down."

"I'm wa—a-a-y ahead of you, inspector. I've just stopped for gas a block from Padonti's place, and hope to find him at his club. Any info on the slug they took out of Steve?"

"Yes, it's a .270 bore rifle. But I have to warn you not to act in your capacity of a private detective. You know damn well that you have to be an officer of the law, otherwise your license is in jeopardy."

"So-o-o;"

"So, right over this phone, I'm deputizing you as an officer of the law. Stay where you are, and I will have detective Hickey return your badge to you pronto. You can take things from there and take him under your wing. Am I right in assuming you've agreed to be deputized?"

"Yes." It was Carver's nature to lighten things up in the face of adversity, so he barged on. "And I'm assuming that by taking up the role pro tem again of detective lieutenant, means I can tear up the last parking ticket and park my Jag—my official police vehicle—in your lot, whenever I please?"

On his agreement, Carver told him his location and looked after priority number two in the men's room.

He returned the key to the pimply-faced attendant on duty, peeled a C-note from the bills in his pocket and handed it and the car keys to the youngster on duty he felt could be trusted.

"I'm being picked up here shortly, young fellow, and should be back within the hour. That hundred will fill the tank with your best, cover an hour's parking and leave you a tip for beer. What's your name? And you *do* have a driver's license, don't you?"

"Yes, sir. I've had a driver's license for two years, an' ain't had no infractions either. My name is Roger Pound."

"Okay, Roger, I'll trust you with things then. Have you got a gun?"

"Yeah, there's one in the drawer by the cash register—you a cop or somethin,' mister?"

"Right on. Anyone gets too interested in that Jag, shoot 'em. And don't park it too close to the car that's parked over there. I don't want to find scratches or dents on that gem when I get back. Do you know who owns that Buick?"

"Yeah, they're a couple of guys what are friends of the guy what owns Gino's Place. One of 'em's big like a house, an' they parks here quite often. The slot's paid for by the year. There ain't much parking on the street near the strip joint."

While waiting in the cool early morning air for Hickey to arrive, *'whom he'd told to get some shuteye'* he took a simple disguise from the glove compartment of his vehicle.

Without the hippy-type wig and floppy hat, the odds of him being recognized in Gino's gathering place for rotten apples, would be too slim to chance. Recognition wouldn't be a concern for detective Hickey, he'd only recently joined the force.

They drove slowly past dimly-lit bars with smoke-stained windows unwashed for years, where the sound of laughter drifted out into the night air on waves of marijuana smoke they could smell out in the roadway.

'Gino's Place' had seen better days when he was kingpin. It had been let deteriorate during his ten years in prison, until recently, when it had been given a face-lift.

Carver figured he surely wouldn't be alone, probably partying to make up for lost time in the slammer. And very likely with some newly installed lieutenants who hoped his contacts with the underworld hadn't diminished in the time he'd been put away.

As Hickey turned into a lane a half block from the club, two black-and-whites, each with two uniformed officers, came from out of nowhere to park behind Hickey's unmarked car. Undoubtedly backups ordered by Inspector Conroy, Carver assumed.

"Stay out of sight close by, fellows," he instructed on going over to the officers, "but be ready for action if I activate a gizmo I've been given by detective James Hickey. It will alert the one that's attached to Sergeant O'Malley's belt."

"Hello there, me buy," was the sergeant's familiar Irish lilt that came Carver's way.

"And hello to you, sergeant. Keep things alert out here."

"Yuh can count on it, me buy."

At this early hour of the morning the area was a hotbed of activity. Freighters were being loaded and unloaded at a series of docks by monstrous cranes that towered into the night sky. The containers captured in their jaws, at this distance replicated miniature toys.

In the chain-link fenced yards and on the outer roadways, huge trucks groaned and squeaked and squealed under heavy loads. It sounded like an out-of-tune symphony; a cacophony of horns and human voices crying out for any number of reasons.

In the street fronting this panorama of life, seamen from ships in port and those anchored off shore, wandered about like lost sheep. They talked in groups, in pairs, hailed cabs anxious to return to loves, find someone to love, or lose themselves in the maze called Los Angeles.

After being tapped a twenty for the cover charges, Carver remarked to the big-busted floozy wearing enough makeup to repair the cracks in the plastered wall behind her; "Must be a good show."

She flashed him a smile. "You'll like it, mister, but if yuh don't," she hastened to add, "*I can give yuh a private showin' later.*"

Carver smiled. "Thanks. I'll pass on that, but my friend here might be interested." He nodded in Hickey's direction.

James Hickey displayed a sense of humor he'd kept hidden up to now. He grinned at the woman and said virtuously, "He's just angry with me, 'cause I smiled at another man last night. We're lovers, you know." He smirked and followed a chuckling Carver into the building.

Standing in back of the smoke-filled club legally capable of seating four hundred patrons, they observed the action while they cased the place. Drug pushers were doing a land office business with impunity, moving about without fear of interruption from the law.

On a stage at a far end of the dimly-lit room, two buxom female strippers were taking it all off, accompanied by canned music from a nearby jukebox.

Gathered round the elevated stage like children enraptured by a puppet show, a collection of off beat dudes three and four deep, higher than kites on any number of substances, whooped and hollered ever louder as each stripper revealed more of what they'd come to play with in their dirty little minds.

It didn't matter that they were being knowingly fleeced, paying exorbitant prices for watered-down drinks, snacks and what have you.

The air was so thick with the sweet stench of marijuana, one hardly needed to shoot up on the hard stuff. At this level of so-called society, man surely didn't live by booze alone. The credo was: *'Live for the moment; a hearse doesn't have a trailer-hitch to tote what might have been.'*

After locating a small table in back of the room, near the bar, which was simply a wall opening through which the waiters ordered; they sat on hard oak chairs and waited to be served.

During ten minutes in which no waiter appeared to clean the table or take their order, Carver observed and pointed out to Hickey, through a haze of cigar, cigarette and marijuana smoke, the club's owner.

He was climbing the stairwell against the far wall of the enormous room, to the second floor landing, where he entered his office. "His living quarters are on the opposite side of that landing, James," Carver pointed out. "Now that I know he's here, I'll create some kind of commotion that'll cause him to remedy the situation. That's what he used to do ten years ago, when he was on tap as both owner and bouncer. He ran the place with an iron fist."

After waiting about fifteen minutes for service, a mountain of a man appeared at their table. He had no neck, a small, clean-shaven head, and towered over them wearing a look that said he was anything but happy with his job. "What'll it be?" he barked.

"Scotch rocks in a clean glass." Carver indicated the messy table with an outstretched hand. "And would you mind cleaning this table of the slop, the dirty glasses and ashtray?"

"I'll have the same," James Hickey spouted like a seasoned drinker, "and I'd also like that in a clean glass."

The waiter didn't respond in any way, he simply walked off and returned about ten minutes later to plop two drinks on the table. He picked up a twenty, said he'd be back with the change, was about to leave when Carver sipped his drink and held up his hands like a traffic cop.

"We ordered Scotch, rocks, this is bourbon. And would you please, clean the table?"

First came a sardonic grin, and then: "Yeah, well, drink it anyway, I sometimes get things mixed up."

As he walked off, Hickey studied Carver's reaction with the concern a mother bear shows for its cub. He'd been told by Steve Holgate that Carver could get real nasty at times, but hardly a muscle twitched on Carver's face. An avid hockey fan, Hickey simply waited for the puck to drop.

The smoke-filled room had reached bedlam proportions. Cries of: *"Take it off. Take it all off."* from a rowdy group up front seemed never-ending as they salivated with anticipation at viewing in the raw, what they'd been denied while spending weeks at sea. Their cries were now becoming a mantra throughout the room.

It was during this commotion that Carver went to the bar and firmly tapped their waiter on the shoulder to gain his attention.

The gargantuan-like fellow turned to confront whomever it was, saw it was his last customer and said rather loudly, "Piss off."

Carver grinned at him, stiffened the fingers of his right hand into a sheet of steel and jabbed the creep exceedingly hard in the pit of his stomach. A painful sounding, elongated "Ug-g-g," ensued, and the waiter's legs folded up like a poorly pegged tent in a windstorm. He dropped to the floor at Carver's feet.

The bartender appeared as though frozen in time as Carver picked the waiter from the floor by the collar of his jacket. The hold tightened to the point the waiter's eyes all but popped while Carver said very quietly, "Two Scotch-rocks, in clean glasses, onto a cleaned table, please." Having said his piece, he returned to the table and was met by an amused stare.

"You are hell on wheels, Carver Frye," James Hickey stated while shaking his head in wonder. "Steve Holgate mentioned it, and now that I've seen it first hand, he didn't exaggerate. But I think you should know that the barman has been having an animated yammering to someone on the phone, while pointing to this table. Maybe your actions have shaken the rafters enough to bring the boss man into the picture."

I hope that's the case, but only you will be sitting at this table if he comes. I'm ducking into the crowd milling about. If he arrives, keep him occupied with anything that crosses your mind. When he least expects it, I'll have my .45 stuck in his ribs. He'll be packing a gun, I'm sure of it."

While detective Hickey sat there awaiting developments, within seconds of Carver walking off through the smoke-filled room, Hickey saw three men leave the office and head down the stairs against the far wall.

That was the last he saw of them until they emerged through the throng of people milling about with drinks in their hands and smoking whatever, to stand looking down at him.

"That ain't the guy, Gino," the barkeeper spouted in the next instant when he arrived on the scene. "He was wearin' a crush hat an' long hair what stunk."

Having removed the basic disguise, Carver came up behind Padonti wearing a smug look and stuck the muzzle of his .45 in Gino's ribs. "Howdy friend, you packing heat?"

The look that came upon Gino at seeing Carver, and those exchanged between the two suits who'd arrived there with him, was one of total disbelief. However, they simply stood their ground and looked on.

Eyes ablaze with anger, Gino spouted in broken English, "What's it to ah you if I'm ah packin' a gun, Frye— I don't report t'no private eye. So screw off. An' what's you an' yer sick-lookin' friend doin' here, anyway?"

Hickey got to his feet and flashed his police badge. "Answer the question, are you packing a gun?"

While Hickey held the spotlight, Carver pressed the call button in his pocket, holstered his Beretta, flipped open Padonti's jacket, saw the gun in the holster under his arm, removed it and snapped the cuffs on the convicted felon. He inspected the piece, removed the shell clip and placed the empty gun into Hickey's outstretched hand.

Seemingly unconcerned up to this point, the two suits suddenly drew their guns. While one aimed his piece at Carver and Hickey, the other guy let loose two shots at the feet of two young fellows from a nearby table, who'd gotten to their feet and looked about ready to enter the fray.

But on being met with the dictum: "Take off you guys if yuh wanna live, an' leave your women right where they are," drew a moment's hesitation, which caused another shot in the area of their feet.

Pandemonium in the room flamed higher as the two young fellows looked on with concern for their female companions. Another shot near their feet found them moving off quickly into the milling crowd, now alarmed with ever-increasing fear at the sound of gunfire.

The suit holding the gun on Carver and Hickey, backed away to join his partner, who'd taken hostage one of the women seated at the table with the two fellows who'd been forced to flee the scene.

On tracking backwards toward an Exit door onto a lane, guns leveled at the detectives; they opened it, fired their guns again to create more panic, abandoned their hostage and left on the run to intermingle with a crowd of frightened patrons running helter-skelter, hell bent on getting out of harm's way,

The room had become absolute bedlam as Carver and Hickey looked on, helpless to do anything but observe.

Women were screaming from fear, while men in varying stages of it and inebriation, scurried about trying to get their women out of harm's way.

They toppled tables containing glasses full and empty, ashtrays, snack-foods, burning cigars, cigarettes, butts and whatnot, while hollering from fright at the top of their lungs. Adding to this was the loud music emanating from the jukebox, accompanied by the sounds of breaking glass as chairs were heaved through windows to set up escape routes.

The backdrop of curtains on the stage abandoned by the strippers, had burst into flames, and the hysteria heightened as patrons headed in droves for the broken windows and other exits.

The onrush of people headed for the exits, was a tour de force that was unstoppable, as they moved past the contingent of officers Carver had summoned at the push of a button. They could do little more than look on.

Carver and Hickey glanced at one another wearing subdued grins. There'd been no point in attempting to chase down the suits who'd taken the woman hostage. Their flight during the donnybrook they'd created had succeeded.

Were it not for the well-dressed suits who'd been in Gino's company packing weapons, and probably had records; there'd have been no need if they were clean to take the hostage, flee the law and create the havoc they had.

Leaving James Hickey in charge of Padonti and give instructions to close the club, Carver went on a search of the premises in hopes of finding the .270 bore rifle that had been fired at Steve. He found nothing of the sort in the office, or in Padonti's living quarters at the top of the stairs.

Chapter 10

TWENTY past four in the morning, Hickey and Carver left the ransacked, fire-scarred, closed-up club, and drove the block to where Carver's new blood-red Jaguar convertible had been left.

On the rear seat of detective Hickey's unmarked sedan, sat fifty-year-old Gino Padonti, hands cuffed behind his back in discomfort, wearing a face livid with rage.

The lights that had illuminated the gas bar, the attendant's glassed-in quarters with all manner of goods a traveler would need, the service islands and the floods atop the metal poles to light the property, were out. The place was closed.

Carver turned to Hickey. "Something sure as hell is wrong here. These places are open around the clock. My car is still here, but why is the place closed and where would the attendant be with my keys?" Hickey drove to the glassed-in enclosure and shut the motor off.

They got out to look around, Carver to his Jag, hoping the keys would have been placed atop a tire, nothing there. He sauntered back to the enclosure to see Hickey peering intently inside, hands cupped to his eyes to eliminate glare.

"Take a look," Hickey said in a concerned voice and stepped aside.

After adopting the same tactic to view inside, sure enough, the young attendant Roger Pound, to whom Carver had entrusted his car keys, was lying face up in a pool of blood.

His body was wedged against the bottom of the heavy, metal-clad entrance door, and the protruding base of a counter.

Carver turned to Hickey with more than just concern for his car keys written on his face. "It looks to me like the young man was killed in a robbery. He told me there was a gun in the drawer alongside the cash register, but from the looks of things, he never got to use it. The drawer's open, but no gun. You've obviously tried the door, James."

"Yes. It moved inward very little, regardless of how hard I pushed, so I came back here to have a better look."

They returned to what was a solidly constructed metal-framed entrance door, and after a joint effort were able to move it ajar just enough to squeeze through and step over the young man's body.

Hickey flicked on the breakers of a control panel and the property was again alive.

On checking the murdered attendant's pockets, Carver found an unsigned note wrapped around his car keys. As Hickey looked about, Carver read the note:

'I closed up the joint, took your car for a run, and just made it back before the car conked out as the battery went dead.'

Carver looked skeptical, and held the note out to his partner. On reading it, James Hickey returned the note and stated: "It's hard for me to believe that a battery would go dead on a new car in such a short time."

"That's also my concern, James. I'm going to check out this handwriting."

Sure enough, after comparing the handwriting of the note with the young man's signature when he signed for a cash float of one hundred dollars, the handwriting wasn't the same.

"Hand me one of the envelopes from the counter, James. Unfortunately, this note is evidence we've unsuspectingly contaminated by handling it. But that was unavoidable, given the circumstances."

He placed the note in the envelope and put it in his jacket pocket. On glancing at Hickey he saw him wearing a frown, as though pondering something. "What's bugging you?" he asked.

"You said earlier, that based on your experience, the state of the victim's blood puts the time of the killing at around three this morning. That's the time when all hell broke loose at the club and those two suits took off. A car that you say was parked over there is gone, and your leather key container, a gift from your dealer, has your name embossed in gold. Think about that."

"I can't, at the moment. It's been a long day, and I'm dog tired."

"Anyway, Carver, I'll go out to my vehicle and call in what we've found here. Soon as the forensic boys and the coroner arrive, we can get back to the precinct with our friend Padonti and start some serious questioning."

"The hell you say! Maybe you didn't hear me, I'm pooped. Ever heard of something called sleep? It's five in the morning, damn it. The questioning of Padonti can wait. That fat slob can park his ass for the night on a hard cell bunk."

"Yep, you're right. I'm tired, too." Hickey stepped over the body, squeezed through the restrictive metal door opening, got out onto the raised cement walkway and immediately shoved his head and hand back inside. "We've gotta get your wheels going. Toss me your car keys. Maybe the battery will turn over now. I'll check it out after I report in to headquarters."

"Thanks." Carver tossed him the keys.

The moment Hickey caught them a gasoline tanker pulled onto the lot and came to a pulsating stop behind where Carver's Jaguar had been parked.

The driver got out of the cab, spotted Hickey and called out, "Any idea who's the owner of this car? It's blocking the filler caps to the underground tanks."

"Yeah, my friend inside the office owns it. We're detectives with the L.A.P.D." Hickey showed his badge. "I've got to report what looks like a robbery and murder. So, here's the keys." He tossed them to the truck driver. "The battery might be dead, but give it a try. If worse comes to worst, we can always push it out of the way." In his next breath he said: "Why in hell are you making a delivery at this ungodly hour of the morning?"

"Best time, officer. Traffic is thinned out on the freeways and in the city, we've got more room to maneuver these big rigs."

When Carver finished his search of the small office and sales cubicle for clues, he glanced from the window at the burly driver looking longingly at the keys to the Jaguar in his hand.

A great big smile crossed the guy's face as he saw Carver looking from the window, and he called out to Hickey: "If this beauty starts, just might be I'll drive off and leave you guys the tanker."

Hickey chuckled, got into his unmarked police vehicle, and was talking on the phone to headquarters when he looked up and saw the driver get behind the wheel of the Jaguar.

It was at this point that the tired gears in Carver's head began to mesh properly. They told him in the blink of an eye that action was critical. He hammered on the glass in hopes of attracting the trucker's attention, but he was too late.

The instant the trucker turned the key in the ignition, an ear-splitting series of explosions ripped the Jaguar apart in a ball of flames that towered into the night sky, and grew into an ominous black, mushrooming cloud.

Carver was through the door of the cubicle in a flash, running like a being possessed. The heat from the burning Jaguar was a blast furnace gone mad, but he was hell bent on getting to the gasoline tanker that was parked perilously close.

While the driver was being cremated before his eyes, he mentally thanked the fellow for leaving the cab door open and the motor running.

He geared the massive truck backwards, out of harm's way, unaware that he was also grinding the back end of Hickey's vehicle into a pile of junk. When he had time to look in the truck's elongated side mirror to his left, he wondered why Hickey was struggling with the lump of lard that was Padonti, pulling him frantically from the rear seat of his car to the ground.

Arriving on the scene at that moment from a block away, a couple of police cars in the vicinity were drawn there by the series of explosions lighting up the night sky, and were in time to witness Carver turning the rear of Hickey's vehicle into a pile of junk.

On learning what he'd done, after getting down from the tanker's cab, Carver shrugged his shoulders as if to say, "What the hell, nobody's perfect."

As a group, Hickey and the officers who'd arrived on the scene, began to applaud. This happenstance had Carver completely confused before he realized that in moving the gasoline tanker out of harm's way under such perilous conditions, he really was lucky not to end up like the tanker driver. He had gone to that big truck stop in the sky, behind the wheel of a very expensive Jaguar.

Chapter 11

IT was seven in the morning, some six hours since Carver had agreed to help his ex-partner solve the mind-boggling murder of Morton Bradley.

With Steve in the hospital, having undergone an operation to remove a sniper's bullet that had come perilously close to killing him, he'd added to his workload.

By taking on this temporary assignment as an officer of the law, he was also in charge of fledgling detective James Hickey.

After Hickey reported in, and saw to it that Gino Padonti was in a cell at the 32nd Precinct, Carver had a patrol car officer drop him off at his residence.

After a relaxing shower and a cup of instant coffee, he sat on his bed and phoned Emma Holgate.

"And you just might be next," Emma scolded after they'd discussed Steve's situation. "I saw on CNN this morning, what happened to your beautiful red Jaguar. And there was a news flash about you gunning down four baseless louts who tried to kill you in that underground garage. It's a nasty business you're in, Carver. Anyway, thanks for the call, my phone's been ringing off the hook. Talk to you again soon, love. Bye for now, and stay alert."

He shut down his phone and climbed between the sheets totally exhausted, where the inevitability of Murphy's Law came to play. Habitually, he'd left partially open the vertical Venetian blinds, allowing a little light from outside, into the room. It was a habit he'd nurtured since childhood, when he was afraid of the dark. And as usual, due to the light filtering into the room, after a short period of tossing and turning the room started to spin. Within moments he was asleep.

Five hours later he extinguished the alarm, yawned extensively, and now fully awake, phoned Margo at the office. She told him that she'd been brought up to date by

Inspector Conroy on Steve's condition: that he was coming along just fine.

He thanked her for this good news, and asked her to pick up from Inspector Conroy the list of demand note debtors to the Bradley estate, found in the safe. And would she do a run down for him on those people?

His next call was to Bill Tuttle, a close friend, car dealer, sponsor and assistant manager of the Little League ball team Carver managed.

The instant Bill came on the line he spouted, "Yeah, Carver, I know why you're phoning. I watch the news. But from the frequency with which you wreck cars, I'd suggest you drop down to a something less expensive. Your insurance company will love you for it. You're all over the news, and—"

"Shut the hell up," Carver hammered in his ear, "you're pushing my button. Just fill the Jag you have on the showroom floor with gas, get one of your flunkies to deliver it to my pad within the next twenty minutes and you've got a sale. You can send me the bill in the mail."

"Ge-e-z-z; wish to hell I'd been sharp enough to buy Starbuck's IPO at twenty-five cents a share. Look out your window in fifteen, and you'll see a powder-blue Jaguar convertible out front."

Silence, and then: "God help me, a powder blue Jaguar? Okay, I'm in a bind, and you've got a deal if that's the only one prepped. But it'll be traded back to you on a British racing green that I'm ordering from you, right now." He closed the call by hanging up before his friend was again infected with verbal diarrhea.

Ten minutes before three, Carver parked his new wheels in the *'Police vehicles only'* lot at the 32nd Precinct. On glancing up to see the inspector looking from his office window wearing a confused grin, he waved at him from the wrist in the fashion of a gay, and smiled inwardly.

Margo met him in the vestibule, having only just dropped off to the inspector her analysis of what Carver had asked for, dealing with the debtors who owed the larger amounts to the Bradley/Spencer partnership.

She put a hand to his neck and kissed him on the cheek. "At least you're still in one piece, and I like that, Carver. But that new car?—it's really not you, although it fits the antics I saw you display on coming into the building. Who were you waving at?"

"Inspector Conroy. We're lovers, you know," he said, taking a page from Hickey's book, and repeated the hand antics.

"That'll be the day." She smiled, told him she'd left with the inspector the details on the larger loans, wished him luck on his imminent interrogation of Padonti, and left the building smiling profusely at his sense of humor.

The bare walls of the interrogation room were a drab gray. A sink was in a far corner, and a droplight hung suspended in the center of the room, above a table with four hard-backed chairs. The room was wired to record what was being said, which could be heard by those looking on through a one-way glass mirror.

Having spent a sleepless night, Padonti looked drawn and agitated when he entered the room under escort, and told to sit at the table.

The escorting officer left the room and closed the metal-clad door with a resounding bang that sounded somewhat final. After ten minutes of being alone with his thoughts in this bleak environment, Carver and Hickey entered the room and caught Padonti picking his nose.

Coming up to the table, Carver snickered. "I'd bet that you eat those delicacies, Padonti."

"Up ah yours," the felon spat in his usual heavy accent as Carver sat at the table. "I heard you was back on ah the force." Padonti chuckled. "Couldn't make it as a private eye? That's easy t'figure, yer too ah stupid." Having said his piece, he leaned forward and spit on the table in front of Carver.

A reflex action saw Carver reach out and slap the felon so hard on the face, he fell from the chair to the floor.

Hickey, who'd been standing nearby, helped the corpulent felon back onto his chair while the imprint of a hand glowed on Gino's face and hatred burned eternal in his eyes.

Carver looked disdainfully at him. "I want you to tell us where you were last night, between one and two A.M., and who was with you."

On reading the stolid expression on the detective's face, the felon readily responded. "I was in my office at ah the club, from maybe eleven o'clock until you come along with this officer." He nodded in Hickey's direction. "I'm ah there talking with a couple fellows about borrow money to fix up ah the club even better. I order a pizza, maybe one in ah the morning. We take ah the delivery from Tony's Pizza, down ah the block."

Hickey nodded at Carver and left the room.

Carver continued. "Where did you get the money to fix up the club, six months before your release from prison?"

Padonti glared at his interrogator a lengthy time. "I don't have ah to tell you. That's, a private matter."

Carver grinned. "What time was that again when the pizza was delivered?"

"Must ah be like I said, maybe one, one-thirty in ah the morning."

Hickey returned and placed a note into Carver's outstretched hand that read: *'His alibi stands. The owner of Tony's Pizza I spoke with on the phone, says he delivered the pizza himself on his way home, at close to one-forty in the morning, to the best of his recollection. That Gino paid for it with a twenty, which left a five-dollar tip. He says the pizza was a large, with double cheese and lots of anchovies.'*

Padonti appeared unsettled while waiting for the detective he'd sworn to kill, adjudicate on his chances of going back to prison for the gun violation.

Carver pocketed the note. His face expressionless, he said, "You are free to get your ass out of here, Padonti."

The detectives returned to Steve's office, where Hickey confronted his superior while they drank coffee.

"Why did you let him go? You didn't ask him about the two hundred thousand I show him owing the Bradley/Spencer partnership. Nor did you ask who the suits were who took that woman hostage. And the fact he's a convicted felon found packing a gun, never came up. Why?"

"Simply put, James, Gino wouldn't have cared a rat's ass if I'd grilled him all night about the hostage takers who did the shooting to create a diversion for their escape. And the amount he owes the partnership has no bearing at all, as to who it was took that shot at Steve Holgate."

"Well, you're the boss," Hickey moaned, "so I guess we're doing things your way."

"Well said, James. And you won't see me flash a badge unless I have to. I can get more done on my own, than a whole carload of detectives tied to a set of regulations. And packing a gun in contravention of the rules, would maybe get the creep a slap on the wrist. The prisons are overloaded as it is. No, Gino is better left to screw up on his own again, and I'm convinced he'll do that sooner than later." He smiled briefly at Hickey. "What's your take on this shot at Steve, any ideas come to mind, James?"

"No, nothing, other than Padonti's statement that's on record to get both you and Steve Holgate when he got out of prison."

"Do you happen to recall the similarities in builds, and the outer clothing worn by Steve and Victor Spencer?"

"Yes I do, now that you mention it." Detective Hickey pursed his lips in a thoughtful mode and nodded his head knowingly. "Then you're saying, the sniper meant to kill Bradley's partner, Victor Spencer?"

"Right on, James Hickey. I'm going out to the Bradley residence to take another look at that study. The impossible just doesn't happen. Meanwhile, find out who it was that built the Bradley spread."

"Okay, but you're wasting your time looking over that study again. Experienced forensic people, including you and Steve Holgate gave it your all."

It was nearing four-thirty this sunny afternoon when Carver parked beside the fountain. On hearing the sound made by a sprung diving board and the splash when someone got wet, he made for the crushed limestone pathway he'd observed earlier, which led to the pool and tennis court area.

After emerging from a wall of flowering shrubs and trees that created privacy for the area, he stopped short to fully appreciate what he'd come upon.

As with everything else he'd seen at this residence, the pool, cabanas, the gardens and all else, fitted the impeccable tastes of its now dead owner.

The soon-to-be owner, Mrs. Lillian Bradley, stood to inherit a fortune. Bradley's will was in that study safe, along with copious amounts of expensive jewelry, and cash in large denomination bills. Stock certificates of notable corporations, and a host of other documents that needed scrutiny. Was a clue to the murder mystery to be found in this mishmash of items?

He stood on the pool's tiled apron and glanced about while his sight adjusted to the sun's glare on the pool's water.

Lillian Bradley was lying on a spring-filled lounge, wearing a flesh-colored bikini that barely covered enough skin to qualify as a bathing suit.

Her sister, Beverly Hughes, was stroking her way in his direction, to the pool's ladder. She climbed from it, went to a lounge beside her sleeping sister, picked up a towel left lying there, came directly over to him, produced a devilish grin and handed him the towel.

"Hello, Mr. Frye, please dry my back. I recall seeing you with detective Holgate last night. I'm sorry to hear on the news this morning that he was shot. Have you heard if he's all right?"

"Yes, and thank you for your concern. He's a good friend, and I'm happy to hear that he's coming along fine."

"Thank the Lord for that. We were astounded to learn of what occurred here last night. The doctor gave us sleeping pills that knocked us out until we woke this morning. Lillian was so distraught at hearing on the TV of her husband's murder, she drank to excess. As you can see, she's sleeping it off on the lounge."

She thanked him for drying her back and offered with an outstretched hand for him to be seated. He sat where she'd indicated at an umbrella table. She came over to it, picked up a bottle of gin standing there and held it out to him. "Might I interest you in a drink, Mr. Frye? There's only tonic water for a mixer, I'm afraid."

"Thanks, but no thanks, Miss Hughes. Gin isn't one of my favorites, not that anything is, but I prefer the taste of Scotch."

"We have that, too, but I'll have to go into the house and search it out. Lillian fired the entire staff this morning. So, using the phone on this table won't prompt anyone to come running."

"I see, well, anyway—I came by to take another look in that study."

She smiled demurely. "Please call me Beverly. And by all means go there, if that's what you came for. Neither I, nor my sister Lillian will go anywhere near that study."

He got up from the table, smiled his adieu, turned and sauntered along a walkway that led to the rear of the mansion.

Its cool interior was comforting and he headed along a lengthy second floor hallway, where he stopped briefly, allowing him to better appreciate the individually illuminated artwork he'd passed by so quickly last night.

At the far end of the hall, recessed ceiling lighting cast an eerie yellowish hue over the massive study door with the heavy, wrought iron hinges spanning almost its entire width. The silence of the house, where not even a whisper of the cooling air could be heard coming from the overhead vents, was an intimidating aura, even to a hardened detective.

He removed the yellow plastic ribbon from the doorframe, declaring the room a crime scene, and unlocked the door using the key Hickey had turned over to him.

On opening the door to see darkness, it was obvious that someone had closed the heavily lined drapes.

He reached beyond the door to press a wall switch he knew was there, but the red-hued pot lamp in the ceiling didn't come on. He supposed it had burned out from yesterday's extended use.

A sniff of the stale air was repugnant and created an anxiety to let in fresh air. On entering the study he quickly headed for the cord that would open up the drapes before unlocking and opening the sliding patio door.

In moving quickly past the antique cherry wood desk, he tripped over something and fell headlong onto the richly carpeted flooring.

In the next instant his heart was in his mouth! Only inches away in front of him, was the stone cold face of Victor Spencer. The unseeing eyes looking at him were filled with pain, as though silently pleading for retribution. His ever present hat lay close by, to disclose that he was indeed bald but for a fringe of gray hair about the ears. His short, rotund body lay in a pool of blood in front of the desk.

He'd been slaughtered like an animal in the forest. A steel-shafted arrow was sticking out of his chest in the area of his heart.

In the dim hallway lighting coming through the open study door, he got to his feet and headed for the pull cord that would open the drapes. On doing so, he released the side and bottom locks on the sliding balcony door, on which a sheet of half inch thick plywood had been attached using screws. He opened it wide, and filled his lungs with fresh air for a full minute, before again entering the room to turn on every light in the study.

He returned to the sliding door and inspected the plywood, to find that it hadn't been tampered with. On the balcony decking again, he took more fresh air deep into his lungs while wondering what Spencer, who obviously had a key, wanted in the room.

There was nothing left in the safe, it had been emptied and left wide open. And nothing of note had been left in the desk drawers.

He reached for his cell phone and reported what he'd found, to Hickey, who'd be bringing the troops along with him. He closed the call saying: "Look for me out at the pool, where the air is fresh, James."

Chapter 12

EXPECTING to find the sisters sipping on gin, he returned to the pool only to find Lillian Bradley there. They hadn't met last night, she'd been too overcome with grief over what, up to that point was a case of domestic battery.

She was sitting up on her sun cot, head slumped forward on a well-endowed chest as though drowsing. In her hand, held at a precarious angle was a partially full glass off what he assumed was gin and tonic. It looked about ready to topple from her grasp.

In slipping it gently from her fingers, she awoke startled, held tightly to the glass through a reflex action and held the drink protectively against her chest.

"Who the hell are you?" came out in an inebriated slur of words while she studied him intently.

"I'm sorry to have frightened you, Mrs. Bradley. My name is Carver Frye. I'm a detective working with the police. You appeared to be sleeping and I was concerned that your drink was about to fall from your hand. I didn't want you to get wet."

A whimsical smile invaded her delicate features before she drained the glass dry in a protracted swallow. "There now, problem solved," she slurred. "I hopes yuh haven't come with more quessions. That detekive, Holygate, I think his name wuz, ashked me so many lass night I wuz becommin' annoyed. Heard on the news thish mornin,' he got hisself shot. Hope he's okay. An' when I heard that my dear husband was murdered, I took to drinkin' an' fired the staff to give me some peace an' quiet."

"Where is your sister, Mrs. Bradley? I spoke with her here about an hour ago."

"She does have a life uv 'er own, detekive Frye. If her Mercedes convertible ain't out front, she'll uv gone t'her aparrment."

Hearing sirens in the distance, she blinked a number of times, took another swig from her empty glass and looked annoyed at seeing nothing there.

"The sirens you hear Mrs. Bradley, will be the police. While taking another look at the study in which your husband was murdered, I discovered the body of his partner, Victor Spencer. He was murdered in the same baffling way as your husband, an arrow through his heart while in the locked study."

The gin soaked expression on her face jumped into shock.

"Do you have any ideas about that, Mrs. Bradley?"

"Lordy, no!" she exclaimed.

"Think your lover would have any ideas about how it was accomplished, Mrs. Bradley?"

"Thass preposserous, I wuz happily married t'Morton Bradley, Mr. Frye. Why would yuh say sush a thing?"

"Then you deny having an affair with Basil Upton, your tennis instructor?"

She manufactured a weak smile that gradually turned into a grin. "So, wuzz so unusual 'bout that in this day'n age? My husband wuz more'n thirty years my senior, Misser Frye. He couldn't pufform in the fuggin' deparrment, so wuzz a girl t'do, sit on 'er hands?"

He was amused by her candor and got to his feet, a smile growing on his face over the arrival of the law. In their usual gaudy fashion they came on the scene lacking only a brass band.

"I'll be back in a little while, Mrs. Bradley. I have a few questions and hope you'll be able to answer them."

"Bye-ye-ye, I'm celebratin' bein' single again." She flicked her eyelids at him before he walked off through what to her, must have been a thick haze.

Returning to the murder room, Carver stood in the doorway observing. It reminded him of a scene right out of The Keystone Cops.

Having visited the room only a few hours ago, the forensic technicians appeared frustrated as they looked about for clues in places already dusted for prints.

A crime scene photographer was again flashing his way through shot after shot, creating the flickering atmosphere attuned to the embryonic days of motion picture art.

Observing Carver's presence in the room, Hickey came over to him and asked, "Did you find what you came looking for when you searched the study again?"

Carver shook his head at the intern and smiled. "Try putting yourself in my place, and see if you can figure the flaw in your question."

After a few moments thought, Hickey produced a weak smile. "Yep, I see it now. Finding Spencer's body put a damper on the search you'd planned. You haven't even started a further inspection of the study."

"Right on. Now let's get the hell out of here. I've had enough of this place for one day. You may as well go home, James. There's nothing more we can do here that we haven't already looked to. I'm going back to the pool and finish up with Mrs. Bradley."

Now closing in on 6:30, the evening was even warmer than yesterday. Arriving at the pool's apron he found the inebriated Mrs. Bradley sitting at the end of the diving board, a drink in her hand, legs dangling above the water like she didn't have a care in the world.

Deeply entrenched in her world, he was certain that she hadn't even seen or heard him return. He sat with the empty bottle of gin on the umbrella table and withdrew the contents of the manila envelope from the inspector, which Hickey had turned over to him.

His main interest at the moment was in the people who owed the Bradley/Spencer partnership the larger amounts of money. The interest rates were a killer, and Margo had checked things out for him in considerable detail.

The name he was hoping to find and did, was that of Lillian Bradley's tennis instructor, Basil Upton. The amount he showed owing was eighty-seven thousand dollars, from an original amount of one hundred thousand.

While his thoughts were immersed in an analysis of what he was reading, a faint rustling of leaves from the other side of a close by hedge of bougainvillea, found his resolve to be cautious had alerted his senses to the fullest.

After the attempts on his and Steve's lives last Saturday afternoon in the park, his encounters with the black Corvette on the street after his Sunday dinner at Dekker's, and the bearded stalker awaiting him while pretending to read a newspaper in the darkened street, the underground parking fiasco at his office building in which four were killed and the Corvette toasted, his red Jag, booby trapped and blown to bits along with the tanker driver, which could have been him, Emma Holgate's warning: *'And you might be next'* was all front and center in his mind. Sure, he was paranoid, who wouldn't be?

He crept silently from where he sat on the pool's tiled decking, to a narrow strip of lawn where there was a slight opening between the dense flowering hedge and a Fan palm.

And, there was his stalker on his knees, the sun reflecting off the gun in his hand as he pretended not to know that Carver was creeping up behind him. The jerk was wearing a crush hat and pretending to pull weeds, when at any moment Carver was aware that he would turn and start blasting away with that gun.

He quickly and silently closed the gap between them and held the muzzle of his Beretta firmly to the guy's temple. "Get up, you son of a bitch! Who the hell are you working for?"

A young fellow of maybe twenty-five, garbed in dark coveralls, stood and turned slowly about to face him while the color drained from his face.

Utterly fearful of what was happening, and in fear for his life while attempting to speak with the cold steel of a gun at his temple, he emptied his bladder while stammering, "I work f-f-or Apex Landscaping, p-p-lease don't shoot me, m-m-mister."

Carver lowered his gun and looked the guy over. Sewn into the fabric of his coveralls was his employer's name. It was then that he realized the guy had wet himself.

"I truly am real sorry, young fellow," he said with marked sincerity. "I guess maybe I'm taking my job of security around here, too seriously."

His lie appeared to lessen the gardener's nervousness, but Carver felt like a fool. He reached into his pocket, peeled a C-note from his money clip and held it out. "Sorry fellah, have a few beers on me." When the gardener didn't take the money, he reached out and stuffed the bill into a top pocket of his coveralls and quickly returned to the pool area.

He sat again at the table where he'd been studying the documents from the safe, which Hickey had turned over to him. And there was Mrs. Bradley at the end of the diving board, still holding and empty glass while looking off into space in consultation with her mind.

Within a few minutes of his return, she began swearing like a hooker picked up for plying her trade. He looked up from what he'd been reading to see her toss the empty glass into the pool.

"What's the problem, Mrs. Bradley?" he called out while coming over to the pool.

She got unsteadily to her feet, looked at him devilishly, danced like a pixie to the secured end of the board and fell headlong into his arms.

"You're a go-o-o-d lookin' bugger, detekive Frye." That said, she released her arms from about his neck. The instant her feet touched the tile decking she flitted about like a whirling dervish and plunked her shapely body down on her sun cot. "Ask away, it's quession an' answer time," she blurted.

He looked down at her from the foot of her cot and shook his head in the negative. "Maybe when you've sobered up, Mrs. Bradley."

"No. Ask yer quessions now big boy while I've got me the nerve t'phone an' break off with Basil. He's bigger'n you, yuh know, could twist yuh inta a pretzel in the blink uv an eye."

"Is this the same Basil Upton who owes the Bradley estate some eighty-seven thousand dollars?"

Her eyebrows shot up. "I din know that!." Appearing stunned by this disclosure she got unsteadily up from the lounge and faced him. "I'm gonna phone that bugger right now," she said without slurring her words, and headed for the telephone on the umbrella table.

On her way she lost her balance and staggered like a tightrope walker on the lip of the pool, attempting not to fall into the deep end. She failed.

The sun's glare on the water's rippling surface foreclosed him from seeing her right off. He located her at the bottom after a short time and wondered if she'd hit her head on the tile coping on falling in.

In the blink of an eye he decided she may have, and divested himself of the Beretta, his phone, his wallet, and dove in.

On coming up to her on the pool's bottom, she eluded his grasp and breast stroked underwater to the shallow end.

He surfaced, swam there and followed her sopping wet onto the pool decking.

She dropped down onto her cot and laughed heartily as water squished from his shoes as he went to retrieve the items he'd divested himself of.

Aware that he'd been played for a sucker, he returned sopping wet to where he'd been sitting at the table.

In the next instant she got unsteadily up from her cot, and began dancing about crazily while coming ever closer to him.

As he looked on she unsnapped the top of her extremely brief bikini and toppled onto his lap like a rag doll. Too stunned to move, he sat there with her naked breasts looking up at him.

Aware that she'd passed out, he chuckled while reaching into a damp pocket for his phone. After listening to the recorded message at his office he consulted his watch, saw it was 8:00 P.M. and realized it had been almost four hours since he'd left the precinct after the interrogation of Padonti.

Again he gazed unhurriedly at the practically nude mermaid on his lap and came up with a lapse of memory. For the life of him he couldn't remember Margo's home phone number. His mind still adrift, he felt really stupid before he remembered that his cell had a memory. He placed the call.

Aware of what he'd be asking of her, he chimed rather pleasantly, "Hello, Margo, I hope I'm not interrupting your dinner, but I've got a problem here at the Bradley mansion and could use your assistance as soon as you can get here."

"It's nice to know I'm needed," she said sweetly, "what's the problem?"

He glanced again at the naked beauty on his lap. "You don't want to know. Just get your body over here, please. I'm at the pool, you'll find it."

"And you can't even give me a *hint* of what your problem is?"

"It isn't often I ask for this kind of help, but if you must know, Margo, there's an almost naked Lillian Bradley on my lap. She's passed out cold and soaking wet."

During a momentary silence he envisioned her reviewing in her mind's eye a picture of Mrs. Bradley in today's *Los Angeles Times.* "And if it hasn't already been aired, Margo," he continued, "there's been another arrow murder in the same locked study."

"I'd guess Bradley's partner, Victor Spencer."

"Brilliant, I'll have to make *you* a partner."

"Sounds interesting, and so does your current predicament." After a few chuckles she said, "I'll be there as soon as humanly possible, Carver."

When she hung, up he returned his attention to the beautiful woman who, unless she was involved in the murder of her husband would be a very wealthy and available widow.

Chapter 13

MARGO arrived poolside within thirty minutes of them speaking on the phone. She came up to Carver sitting at the umbrella table perusing documents. When he looked up and smiled at her, she shook her head in dismay of what she'd come upon and went over to check out the woman on the padded sun cot.

Turning back to him, an amused smile grew on her face. "Couldn't you at least have covered her with more than the skimpy swimsuit? And, didn't you tell me on the phone that just her top was missing? How is it the bottom to her bikini and the top, have been placed to cover her?"

He chuckled. "Well, it happened inadvertently while I was struggling to get out of this chair with her passed out on my lap. Somehow my finger got hooked onto a piece of string and, Kazam!. There at my feet was the last hunk of what she'd been wearing."

"Why not cover her with a towel?"

"She's lying on it."

"Ever think to check in the cabanas? Probably loads of them in there." She walked off and returned from the nearest cabana carrying a large towel and a white terrycloth robe bearing the initials L.B. scripted in royal blue.

"Very cleaver, Margo," he remarked after she'd gotten Lillian Bradley into the robe. "Is there anything unusual to your mind, about any of the debtors on Hickey's list?"

She came to sit with him at the table. "Apart from what you already know about Gino Padonti, the only other person in my opinion worth looking into is a fellow named Basil Upton. He's spent jail time for breaking and entering, is a tennis bum who teaches and reportedly is pretty good at his game. He's a womanizer and presently owns outright a posh health club on Melrose Avenue. Why he hasn't paid off the eighty-seven thousand he still owes the Bradley/Spencer partnership is hard to understand, given the rate of interest on his loan. In fact he hasn't reduced the amount of the loan in the last four years. And I couldn't find anywhere in Bradley's records where the interest had been calculated and recorded. Very strange."

"That's certainly interesting. According to Lillian Bradley, he's a big fellow as mean as a junkyard dog and she's about to break up the relationship her husband was concerned about. There's no telling what his reaction will be when she tells him to take a hike, and that's where you come in."

"And how is it that I come into the picture?"

He appeared hesitant to answer and shrugged his shoulders as if ready for a rejection. "I'd like you to stay the night here with Mrs. Bradley. If she wakes up alone in this house and phones him, there's no telling what might happen. I sure don't need another catastrophe on my hands."

She was silent a time while she pondered what he'd disclosed. "So be it. I will stay the night, Carver. I'll phone mother and let her know that I won't be home."

Now that his concerns had been met, he filled her in on what his day had generated, including the absence of any staff at the mansion due to them all being fired by Lillian Bradley.

But he certainly didn't mention his embarrassing incident with the gardener.

The update over with, he carried the sleeping drunk into the house and left Margo to baby-sit the woman he'd deposited on the bed in such a manner, her robe had flopped open. Whereupon, he found himself being proclaimed, incorrigible.

"I'll just be along the hall inspecting the murder room," he informed her while on his way to the hallway door.

"What is it that you're looking for, Carver? I hear the study has been gone over 'till hell won't have it, as they say, by loads of people, including you."

"I really don't know what I'm looking for, but I've convinced me, that the answer to this conundrum is contained within that room. So, while I'm looking for a needle in a haystack and the drunk is sleeping it off, maybe you could look over the contents of that envelope I've left you. See if anything grabs you. I need all the help you can give me."

She grinned. "I may as well, Carver, I don't see anything to read in here but reams of fashion magazines."

At the bedroom door to the hall he turned and smiled his thanks for imposing on her evening, waved a paw at her and left.

Again he removed the police tape from the doorframe to the study, went in, turned on all the lights, opened up the heavy drapes and the sliding balcony door.

In a matter of minutes he'd established to his satisfaction that no secret panels existed. Not in the walls, under the carpeted floor or in the ceiling, which is precisely what the outcome of the forensic team had found.

He then returned to the massive, beautifully carved cherry wood desk, sat on the upholstered leather tilter chair and as was his slovenly habit, garnered from having rented his furnished office with a badly scarred desk top, he plunked his size tens down on a top corner of the very expensive desk.

He looked a slob, his pants and jacket still damp from the swim in the pool were a wrinkled mess, his socks were bunched up at the ankles and the wet suede slip-ons were badly discolored.

For a lengthy time he sat looking at the open safe before he took a penlight from his damp pocket and removed his feet from the desk.

He went to the safe that was empty save for the short plastic rake used for moving stuff about, removed it and again began an examination of the safe's interior.

Finding nothing out of the ordinary, he returned the flashlight to his pocket and began searching with his fingers, running them over its smooth cold steel surface as far as his arm would reach.

Although he was almost six-foot-two and had long arms, he still couldn't reach to the very back of the safe which was bull nosed at the far end, and embedded in the cement wall that also housed the fireplace.

He struggled to reach to the bull nosed end, but couldn't. On removing his jacket to gain that little extra, there still remained about five inches of the tube unexplored by his fingers. On his final try, extending his arm in so forcefully his rib cage ached, he felt what was an almost imperceptible line running around the tube about four inches from the back.

He withdrew his arm, massaged his armpit for a time and picked up the little plastic rake. Extending it into the safe, he pushed on the bull nosed end. The head of the rake snapped off and left him holding a plastic rod about a foot long.

He removed the rake head, and pushed with the rod against the end of the tube. Bingo!—Bingo!—Bingo!. The bull nosed end of the tube moved silently outward on a spring-loaded hinge and opened up completely. As the warm evening air rushed onto his face he smiled and said expressively, *"Son of a bitch."*

He returned to the balcony, and there interrupting the impeccable workmanship of the intermittent stonework covering the cement wall, one of the larger stones of which there were many, stood out at right angles.

He looked right through the safe into the study. Directly in line with the sixteen inch diameter opening was the desk where both Bradley and Spencer had left pools of blood. Bradley had made it to the study door, but Spencer had dropped in his tracks alongside the desk front.

When he pushed lightly on the opened stone, a spring was activated and the bull nosed end of the safe, secured to the stone, went back into place without a sound. It had meshed precisely with a flange that had been machined into the half-inch-thick, case-hardened steel tube. *"Ingenious"* he remarked.

He looked about in the array of smaller stones for the one that would trigger the mechanism when pushed on. And sure enough, a few inches away from the stone that opened up, one about the size of a cut-in-half chicken egg, of which there were many, activated the spring and the safe opened up silently.

The murderer had only to move things about if a clear shot wasn't available. An unlikely circumstance based on the liberal amount of space available in the safe's length and diameter.

After closing the back of the safe he used his penknife to established that the mortar was rubber, abraded to appear like the rest of the mortar surrounding the stones in the decorative, stonework chimney wall.

More than a little elated, he returned to Lillian Bradley's bedroom suite, opened the door and stood for a moment showing a smile before he went in and closed the door.

Margo looked up at him from a comfortable wing chair and read him correctly. "You found something, didn't you," she stated softly.

"That could be, has Mrs. Bradley stirred at all?"

"No, she's out like a light."

"When she wakes up, she'll wonder who you are. But I know you'll explain things after you mention my name. After she sobers up and gets rid of the headache she's bound to have, I'd like you to establish with her which of the pieces of jewelry on Hickey's list, if any, belong to her."

"There's a total of eight pieces on the list, Carver. All of it looks to be expensive based on what detective Hickey has described. That shouldn't be a problem."

"Thanks for doing this, Margo. I've probably ruined your evening. Anyway, I've got things to do so I'll leave you be." He got up from the chair beside her, but she motioned with her hand for him to sit back down.

She grinned knowingly at him. "I could see from the look on your face when you came into the room that you found something in that study. Won't you tell me what you've discovered?"

He was hesitant for a few moments, and keeping his voice low while seated beside her in the bedroom's sitting room, he explained how the murders had been committed.

She sat there spellbound for a few moments. "When you left here an hour ago, Carver, I had a strong feeling that you'd discover something. I can hardly wait to see the look on the inspector's face when you tell him what you've found."

He shook his head in the negative. "What I've discovered is to go no further than your ears and those of my fledgling partner. Can you image the bramble bushes I'd have to negotiate if the murderer got wind of what I've discovered?"

She smiled reverently at him. "Right again, Carver. My lips are sealed."

Chapter 14

THE instant he got behind the wheel of the powder blue Jag parked beside the Bradley fountain, Carver realized that he and Hickey hadn't touched base regarding the contractor who'd built the mansion. Now, in light of his discovery as to *how* the arrows got into a locked and bolted room, the builder's identity was paramount to unearthing the person or persons involved in these heinous crimes.

He phoned Hickey as he drove and got an immediate response. "Did you dig up the builder's name?"

"Yes, I got that info' from the city planning department in a matter of minutes. The contractor is retired and lives in West Covina, about an hour's drive from L.A."

"Have you anything else to report?"

"Yeah, I did a search of our records and came up with a list of the jewelry taken in the unsolved safe robberies, involving the same Titan safe as that installed at the Bradley mansion."

"You're way ahead of me, James. That, and trying to get a handle on this fellow Basil Upton was my next move."

"Why not take the night off for a change, Carver?"

"That's a thought, but I've got a better one. Have a drink and put your feet up for half an hour. It will take me that long to sashay through this traffic to pick you up for dinner."

"Yeah? That's fantastic. I hear *Dekker's is the place to eat.*"

"You're right, but dinner's on me in West Covina. Being as the builder is retired, while I'm on my way, give him a call and arrange for us to meet him at say, ten this evening if that's not too late. If you don't phone me back pronto, I'll know the meeting's on."

"Okay, but what's so important it can't wait until tomorrow? And for your information, I don't drink."

"Okay, to answer your questions in the proper order, what's so important is, I've discovered a hot iron that I don't want to cool. And what do you mean, you don't drink? You ordered Scotch rocks at Gino's Place."

"Yeah, but you didn't see me drink it. I was only trying to keep up with your macho image. So what about this hot iron you mentioned?"

"I'll tell you later."

On the drive to Marina del Rey, where Hickey lived in one of the high rise apartment buildings, Carver felt pleased that they'd gotten along so well.

Standing outside the apartment building's entrance when he drove up, Hickey opened the car door, appeared impressed at seeing the interior up close, said, "Hi," and sat on the passenger seat's soft leather. "So, what's the occasion that's causing you to splurge for dinner, and don't tell me it's to celebrate this new Jag. I'm even embarrassed to be sitting here. We must surely look like a couple of fags. Powder blue?...my God!."

"Simmer down, James, I needed a car in a hurry and this was the only one prepped and ready on my dealer's showroom floor. I'll be rid of it as soon as the replacement I've ordered gets here. Anyway, you've made the appointment and we've about an hour for dinner before we have to meet this builder fellow, Weldon."

"Yeah, he asked what the meeting was about. I told him it was about the Bradley place."

"Very good, James," Carver remarked while glancing in the rear view mirror. "Well now, I'm quite sure that old black Chevy behind us, followed me for quite a distance on the freeway when I was driving to your place. I'm almost sure that's the same car."

Hickey looked back. "It's a woman driving that old Chevy. The passenger's a guy dozing, with a baseball cap pulled low." He looked at Carver while growing a concerned frown. "You know, I believe you're becoming paranoid. You think everyone is trying to kill you."

"Think what you will, my friend. But when tested I revert instantly to self-preservation and can get damn nasty. Anyway, I'll add a new number to the equation we're involved with. Little more than an hour ago I solved the riddle of how those arrows found their way into a locked study to slaughter my client and his partner."

"The hell you say. Then you *did* find something we all missed in that murder room."

After he established an assurance of secrecy, Carver disclosed the ingeniously contrived method of opening a safe from its back while embedded in a decorative stonework, cement wall.

"Now I understand why this meeting with the builder. Whomever it was did the masonry work must have been in cahoots with the supplier of the altered safe."

"Right on, James. And there's no doubt in my mind that the four unsolved Titan safe robberies of a few years back were accomplished the same way."

Hickey appeared upbeat as he glanced at Carver. "I've brought along what I gleaned from the files on those unsolved Titan safe robberies. And I also have a printout of the jewelry items stolen from them but never recovered."

"That's intuitive thinking, the mark of a good detective, James. That's information we need at our fingertips. You're learning. I've asked Margo to establish which if any of the jewelry pieces found in Bradley's safe, belong to Lillian Bradley."

He passed a car he'd been following for miles while preoccupied with talking. The car behind that held his concern also passed and again pulled in behind.

"It would appear that we've attracted some excess baggage James. That old black Chevy is on our tail again."

"She probably likes your eighty miles an hour and doesn't have speed control."

"You may be right, and it could be that I really have become paranoid."

"Who could blame you after what you've been through? We're coming up to the West Covina turn off, let's see if she follows," James Hickey said and continued looking back. "Well now, that's a relief, Carver. She didn't turn off when we did, so that suspicion goes out the window and we can relax while having dinner."

Chapter 15

AT precisely 10:00 P.M. Carver parked the baby blue Jaguar alongside a black Cadillac in Mr. Weldon's driveway. They got out to look around.

Mr. Weldon had obviously accumulated more that a few shekels during his construction days. His home was definitely upper class, high up in the rolling hills of West Covina.

Before Carver could activate the illuminated button at the front door, it opened. They faced a tall gentleman with a full head of gray hair, a pasty look about him. He managed a brief smile and held out his hand to them. Introductions over with he stepped aside. "Please come in, we'll talk in the study."

From its spacious view window overlooking the vast housing developments and the freeway, the myriad red and white lights of cars traveling in opposite directions, appeared as endless columns of space age monsters on the rampage.

"Have a seat on the couch there, gentlemen." Weldon pointed to a button-tufted burgundy leather piece that matched the other seating in the large, graciously appointed room.

Carver smiled at Mr. Weldon. "Thank you for seeing us this late in the evening, sir."

"Yes, well, it is a little late, but what can I do for you?"

"You were the contractor who built the Bradley mansion. I was hoping you would have a record of all the employees who worked on the project, and that we could have that information."

"Is there a particular person you are interested in?"

"Yes, his name is Basil Upton. We have a record of some of what this fellow has been involved in. He took to learning the masonry trade while in prison, but there's a missing slice of his pie that involves seven years." While he was talking, Carver realized that Mr. Weldon's countenance was turning the color of chalk.

The old fellow got up, went to the study door and closed it. "We can talk now, without being overheard. I don't want Mrs. Weldon upset. The name of that man is poison around here."

They didn't interrupt him while he spelled out the reason for their hatred of Basil Upton.

He had worked as a masonry worker's helper after joining Mr. Weldon's prestigious company. In less than a year he'd become a competent worker and allowed to work without supervision. As well, he'd been made a supervisor of the unskilled laborers, was popular with all the tradesmen who came onto the site, and lived on site in a trailer supplied by the company, who also paid him for watchman duties.

Mr. Weldon stopped for a moment and looked more than a little concerned. "I want you fellows to promise not to use this information in any way that will involve our family."

"We agree," Carver said.

"Well, seeking to impress me I suppose, Upton had taken pictures of the project at a certain point. Uninvited, he showed up at our door one evening to show them. That was the occasion when he met our daughter, Margaret, an event I greatly regret.

She was twenty-one at the time, engaged to a prominent industrialist and foolishly accepted a ride into town that evening with Upton, who was extremely attractive to women. Within a week he'd enticed her to his watchman's trailer for a drink that was undoubtedly drugged, where he seduced her and recorded the incident on video. To make a long story short, I paid him ten thousand dollars for the video, otherwise, the footage would find its way into the hands of her fiancé.

After I paid the money I found myself paying out another, twenty thousand dollars for a copy. Well, within a month my daughter had a breakdown and broke off the engagement.

She eventually recovered, married a nice young man two years later and is presently living in the area. Anything you can do to put that fellow Upton where he belongs, Mr. Frye, would place me forever in your debt."

After a few lengthy moments while Mr. Weldon was becoming composed, Carver responded. "Is there anything else you can tell us about this man?"

"Lots, but I don't know of it firsthand. Rumors mostly, and from overhearing the workmen talking."

"Like what?"

"His involvement with drugs, pimping for call girls, strong-arm collections, taking bets on horses, football, basketball, well, anything a bookie would handle he'd provide an on-site service. And I dare not fire him for fear of reprisals. He's the scum of the earth."

"Was he strictly a front man, or running things for himself?"

"I don't really know, detective Frye. There were rumors he was fronting for John Harvey in a high class call girl operation that involved shirts."

"Shirts, and who is this John Harvey?"

Looking surprised Mr. Weldon said, "Yes—shirts. And you really don't know who John Harvey is—or was, I should say? That was an alias used by Morton Bradley."

Carver could hardly believe his ears. In the time he'd been a sleuth with the L.A.P.D., Morton Bradley's public persona embraced a cleanly polished silver-plated image. Except for the loosey-goosey *'information'* about money laundering and loan sharking he'd uncovered in the police files after taking him on as a client, one wouldn't have expected to find rust beneath the silver plating.

"What's this you mentioned about call girls and shirts, Mr. Weldon?"

"I overheard the workmen discussing it at lunch break one day. Seems there's a company called Pal Shirts somewhere close to the shipping docks. The shirts can only be delivered through a call girl who charges what the traffic will bear, and for the shirt worth maybe fifty dollars she gives a receipt for that amount, If I remember correctly. A first time John has to be recommended by an existing client. The fellows mentioned something about knowing the existing client's sleeve length, collar, chest size and color preference. Part of a verifying check system, I don't remember for sure."

Carver smiled warmly at the old gentleman, got to his feet and walked across the room with hand extended.

Wearing a concerned look, Mr. Weldon stood, clasped the outstretched appendage and said, "Remember your and Mr. Hickey's promise now, I don't want the Weldon's involved in any way."

"Mr. Weldon," Carver started off smiling, "thank you very much for your information. And you can rest assured that we will keep our promise."

It was midnight when they waved goodnight to the old gent in the doorway.

Wednesday-June 18

Chapter 16

FEELING elated over the results of their two hour meeting, Carver drove the baby blue expeditiously along a narrow, treed hillside road and headed for the freeway.

Parked beyond their sight on a side road above the narrow road through the heavily-treed hillside, sat an old black Chevy with its motor shut down. A woman seated behind the wheel was twiddling her thumbs while she awaited the return of her passenger.

On the treed embankment above the road being traveled by the Jaguar, a big fellow wearing a baseball cap lay on his stomach behind a fallen tree, on which rested the barrel of an AK-47.

On rounding a bend in the road, the baby blue was met with a hailstorm of bullets that blew out the front tires, shattered the windshield and sent the car airborne over a steep embankment and into the bush and trees at its base, some fifty feet lower down.

§ § § § §

A glossy white ceiling was the first thing Carver observed when he opened his eyes. The antiseptic odor of a hospital alerted his senses and out of concern he looked himself over.

Apart from a gnawing pain in his head, everything appeared in order but for missing the left sleeve of his shirt. It had been replaced by a fresh plaster cast on his arm, from slightly below his elbow, to maybe three inches above the hand joint.

On glancing about he saw that his jacket was a nasty looking mess, hung over the back of a chair. He was about to get up from the bed when the door to the room opened.

A white smock walked in wearing a stethoscope dangling about its neck like a pet serpent. "Well now, you are awake," said the smock. "I'm Doctor Robert Manley of the West Covina Medical Center. How are you feeling, detective Frye?"

"Apart from a lousy headache and this thing on my arm, I'm okay."

With the professionalism of a father figure the doctor smiled at him. "You sustained a hairline fracture of the ulna in your left forearm. I put on a cast and the arm should mend quickly. Just take things easy and don't add to the problem by putting it in harm's way. See your doctor in a couple of weeks, okay?"

"Sure thing, doc, thanks. How's my partner?"

"He has a slight concussion, contusions about the face, head and upper body, and a few minor cuts on his legs, nothing for you to be concerned about."

"I'm sure relieved to hear that. When I dragged him from a blazing inferno that used to be a powder-blue Jaguar, he was unconscious."

Doctor Manley's eyebrows went up on his mentioning the color, but he didn't appeared to be interested in the details and simply said, "We contacted the Los Angeles Police Department about a half-hour ago. They've dispatched a helicopter to return you and your friend to the city. It should be here shortly, and you and your friend are free to go."

The words had only left his mouth when the sound of a chopper overhead made its presence known.

Assisted by a burly intern, Hickey walked unsteadily toward the chopper and was helped aboard. The pilot buckled him in while Carver climbed in unassisted, sat alongside Hickey and settled back to drowse and count his blessings.

When the chopper was on the ground at the 32nd Precinct parking lot, it was met by Inspector Conroy and a small group of officers who'd drawn the early morning shift.

The instant Carver's feet touched terra firma the inspector confronted him. "Good God, I can't tell you how relieved I am that you two weren't killed in that car crash. What were you fellows doing in West Covina, anyway? And how is the investigation going? The media is constantly on my back looking for answers. You sure as hell don't keep me or anyone else informed. Surely you can give us something of a progress report. Steve is coming along just fine, and as a matter of fact they've got him up and walking already. It's, bloody well amazing what the doctors are doing these days."

He stopped to take a breath while the others looked on. When finally he noticed the cast on Carver's arm his mouth came alive again. "What, you've broken your arm? The doctor didn't tell me *that* over the phone. Surely you'll be able to continue working on this case, Carver."

All the while he was running off at the mouth, Carver and Hickey stood there looking like they'd done battle with a pride of lions protecting a kill. Their clothes looked fit for the garbage dump, being filthy dirty, ripped, torn, scorched and burned.

In no mood to listen to more of the inspectors yammering, Carver cracked a pained grin and said quite rationally, "I know this may sound somewhat logical, inspector, but maybe you could bring things into focus. After our ordeal, detective Hickey and I would probably like to get into our beds for a rest. A couple of squad cars to drive us home should fill the bill, wouldn't you think?"

§§§§§

An annoying ache in his left arm woke Carver. He glanced at the bedside clock, 9:00 A.M. He was still fully dressed in the filthy clothes he'd arrived home in, his slip on shoes in a corner of the room. He rubbed his eyes open and headed for the bathroom.

Twenty minutes later he emerged naked as a plucked turkey from a cloud of steam, wearing a hand towel wrapped firmly around the cast on his arm to keep it dry.

Seated on a side of his bed he dialed his car dealer. The switchboard operator knew his voice well, and as usual would alert her boss as to who was calling.

"Morning, Carver," Bill Tuttle started off before Carver could utter a word. "Glad to know that you're still in one piece. The television coverage this morning had a shot of your baby blue, front and center. I've a call in to your insurance company, but I'm afraid they might insist I don't write up any more of your insurance business."

"You smart ass. I'll bench your kid and won't let him pitch for the next ten games. Did you get my check for the baby blue?"

"No."

"That's good, because I haven't written it yet."

"You smart ass."

"What's on your showroom floor?"

"Another Jag, this one's a silver-gray, want me to send it over?"

"Why not, half an hour's soon enough."

"What else, you're always in a hurry. It'll be there in a half, Buddy."

Carver hung up and listened to messages from Helen Dekker. The first was: "Give me a call, big boy; I haven't talked to you in a week. Charles tells me you were in for lunch with that ravishing partner of yours I've never met. You and Margo are invited for dinner at the house, Saturday evening. Come early, dinner's at eight, and I won't take no for an answer."

A second call made while he was showering, said: "Carver, this is me again. What in hell are you doing that you're in so many scrapes lately? I know you're busy and I haven't wanted to bother you, but the news in the last couple of days showed your new blood red Jaguar bit the dust in an explosion and fire, where a gasoline tanker driver was killed. And now, just a few minutes ago, I'm tuned in to the news and what else, another new Jag you apparently bought like hours ago was blown to bits out there in West Covina of all places. Give me a call, love.

Charles says I have to have a long talk with you about leaving these arrow murder investigations strictly in the hands of the police. Don't forget now, we'll see you and Margo on Saturday for dinner, bye."

He observed the weather through his always partially open vertical Venetian blinds. A habit he'd continued with since growing up as a youngster in the town of Wilmette, on the shore of Lake Michigan, a short distance from Chicago.

He dressed in a suit tailored to accommodate an under arm holster, and as luck would have it, the rock hard cast on his forearm not being bulky, it was unlikely of even being noticed.

.

He plucked the phone from its cradle and dialed Lillian Bradley's number. "Hello," said a vibrant, sexy voice that could bring a dead battery to life.

"This is detective Frye, Mrs. Bradley. How are you feeling this morning?"

"Fit as a fiddle and anxious to play," she quipped.

'*Hardly the attitude of a grieving widow,*' he thought and grinned into the mirrored base of the lamp on his nightstand. "That's a pleasant surprise, Mrs. Bradley. Would Miss Sanchez happen to be close by? I'd like to talk with her."

"Yes, she's right here. And if she's your lady friend, I'll have to stop thinking about you. She's a catch, and you'd better not let her get away. But maybe I should mind my own business. Anyway, detective Frye, I want to thank you for having her stay the night with me. There's no telling what I'd have done had she not been here. Probably, I'd have phoned that big lug Basil and told him to go screw himself."

He was amused by her attitude and her observations about Margo, and heard her pass the message along that Mr. Frye would like to talk with her.

"Hello, Carver, Mrs. Bradley has gone back into the bathroom and closed the door, so we can talk. I notice she's had her eye on you, as have I, constantly, I'll have to admit. But she didn't remark that we learned over the morning news, about your ordeal in West Covina. It must have been a horrible experience. And I've been thanking the Lord, that you and detective Hickey are alive."

While she was talking, he was exceedingly pleased to hear her openly admit that he was in her thoughts. And while his concerns about the attempt on his life where ongoing, he made light of it.

"Yeah, well, as you know, those are the breaks in this business, Margo. Anyway, the meeting with the contractor who built the Bradley mansion went well. Have you established if any of the jewelry on Hickey's list belongs to Mrs. Bradley?"

"Yes I have, Carver. Seven of the eight pieces are hers. She says that her diamond brooch, similar to the item she didn't tick off as belonging to her, is missing. That the center diamond on her brooch was a three-carat stone. The one detective Hickey recorded as being in the safe has a five carat stone and isn't hers, she says."

"Well now, another mystery. A missing brooch replaced by one that's more expensive."

"It looks that way. But it's possible the one she says isn't hers may have been held as security on one of the loans. I'll check that out as soon as I get back to the office, Carver."

"Thanks, Margo. That's something we have to know, but it still leaves us with a missing brooch. It's possible that Mrs. Bradley has it in a drawer and hadn't yet given it to her husband to be returned to the safe."

"Yes, that's a possibility. I'll do a search with her before I leave. And she has another concern I should mention. She phoned her sister this morning to confirm they'd be meeting at their hairdresser's and go for lunch after they got prettied up. But her sister Beverly doesn't answer the phone. The concierge at her apartment tower checked. He reported that she was not in her suite and her car was not in her parking slot in the secured underground facility. He said that he hadn't seen her since Sunday afternoon. That's when she came to visit Lillian, here at the mansion."

"Hum-m-m," Carver mused. "I met Beverly Hughes Monday afternoon at the pool, when Lillian Bradley was bombed out on gin. Maybe she'll show up at the hairdresser's shop. Oh-h," he said as a precursor to changing the subject, "did I happen to mention we are invited to the Dekker residence for dinner, Saturday night?"

"No, you didn't, but I'd like that. I guess mother will have to eat alone for a change."

"All right then, I'll pick you up in my new Jag, say about seven on Saturday?"

"Another, Jaguar!" she exclaimed. "That's three different cars in about the last forty-eight hours. Anyway, Carver, seven Saturday night is fine with me."

"Good. Has Mrs. Bradley emerged from the bathroom yet?"

"Yes, she's just come out."

"Put her back on the line, will you?"

A slight pause, "Yes, Mr. Frye, what is it now?"

"Are you still of a mind to break off with your friend Basil Upton?"

"Yes, definitely. I intend phoning him shortly."

"Why not tell him to his face, Mrs. Bradley?"

"Are you kidding me, he'd bat me from one wall to the next."

"Not if I was there with you."

A short silence. "Why not, hear tell from Ms. Sanchez that you're a black belt in karate and judo. Could be an interesting encounter. Basil has won prizes in body building contests, knows karate and has a short fuse. Sure. I'd like to see his response on being face to face with someone like you. But it will have to be about three this afternoon, after my hairdresser and luncheon appointment with my sister. He's usually there at his club, he lives there."

"All right then, don't phone and tell him that you are coming. We can meet at his health club parking lot at three this afternoon, is that agreeable to you, Mrs. Bradley?"

It was and he hung up the phone. There was much on his mind today, but first things first.

At his kitchen counter he took apart his Beretta, cleaned and oiled it thoroughly. Back on the phone again he got Hickey on the first ring. "If you feel anything like you sound, James, you'd better take a whole bottle of whatever it is they say perks you up. Are you still a little groggy in the head after last night?"

"I feel all right, had a good sleep. What's on our plate for today?"

"I don't know about you, but I'm thinking of a different kind of plate at the moment. It's called a late breakfast. Think you can make it to Mary's joint where we had pie yesterday afternoon, maybe in half an hour or so?"

"Okay, you don't have wheels, so I'll pick you up on the way."

"Negative, James. I've got me a silver bullet waiting out front that my car dealer says is a pant remover par excellence."

"What, another Jaguar convertible?"

"Yeah, see you in a half. If you're late I'll start without you."

Hickey was two minutes short of a half hour when he arrived at the cafe'. Greetings and superlatives about the new Jag out front over with, they were soon presented with the substantial breakfast Carver had described over the phone. But before it arrived, Carver engaged the attention of his partner.

"I'd like to get down to figure where we're going on this murder investigation I've been roped into."

"You've got that wrong. I recall you saying to Steve Holgate that wild horses couldn't keep you from this case."

"Yeah, but at the time only Bradley had been murdered."

"So now you've got something you can really get your teeth into. Want me to spell it out for you?"

"Sure, as an up and coming detective, let's hear your thoughts on some of the loose ends."

For the next few minutes Hickey rehashed what they did and didn't know, including his speculation that the guys who fled Gino's Place were the one's who'd parked at the gasoline service station. On seeing Carver's name embossed on the leather key case in the attendant's possession, they'd killed the kid with the gun that was there, rigged the Jag's starter with a bomb and planted the keys along with the note. The logic being that Carver would try to start the car and check out the battery himself. But it was the driver of the tanker who got toasted. And, through those two wearing their hat brims turned down low, he couldn't waste his time looking at mug shot files.

"Not bad, James. There's some wild speculation in there, but it could have been an ugly scenario somewhat of that nature. Anyway, we have to learn the name of the guy who installed the Titan safes in California, and check out the houses where the same make of safes were robbed a few years back, and remain unsolved in police files. That's on our plate the soonest, James. Margo has learned that seven of the eight jewelry pieces described on your list, belong to Mrs. Bradley. The eighth piece is a brooch with a five carat center diamond, that doesn't fit with the three carat diamond in Mrs. Bradley's brooch, which is missing."

"That's sure interesting, but the five carat diamond brooch, doesn't fit with items stolen in the unsolved Titan safe cases."

"Okay, that question is eliminated. Now Mrs. Bradley's sister, Beverly, is missing. They arranged a luncheon meeting for this afternoon, we'll wait and see if she shows."

"So that's about it?"

"Almost, but not quite. I've some sophisticated listening equipment I intend placing in the bathroom within Padonti's office. It activates automatically to record conversations within that room and the office. I can punch in a code from a block away and hear what's been recorded. It's the size of a replacement roller, used to dispense toilet paper."

"Hum-m, interesting, I don't suppose that you've obtained a court order to install that device."

Carver grinned. "If you don't know the answer, you can't be lying if asked."

"You're right. What else is a priority in the scheme of things?"

"The call girl business Mr. Weldon spoke of. And I expect to have a meeting with Basil Upton this afternoon. Mrs. Bradley will be telling him that things they had planned have hit the off button. It'll be interesting to see his reaction."

"You surely are burning a hole in the ten grand Bradley sent you."

"That's a fact, but I'll be placing a call to the head honcho of Titan Iron & Steel in Chicago, to learn what its worth for them to get their Titan safes back onto world markets."

"I see. If one of their technicians is involved and you can prove a case of safe tampering against that person, it could earn you back the ten grand."

Carver chuckled. "Elevate your sights, James, I don't work for peanuts. Each installer is undoubtedly insured against dishonesty to the tune of at least a million dollars. And ten percent of that amount would not be an unreasonable figure to start negotiations."

"Wow."

"Wow, indeed. But this stuff is to go no further than your ears."

"I hear you, but the inspector is on my back constantly to tell him something that will get the media off his back."

"The less he knows the better. I never knew a cop shop that could keep things under wraps for long, one of the reasons I left the force."

"Well, we're done with breakfast, so I'll get to work to prove your theory that each unsolved Titan safe robbery in the residences I'll be looking at is a clone of the situation at the Bradley mansion."

"Yes. And the reason I believe the Titan technicians couldn't find any flaws when they inspected those safes, is because no flaws existed. A proper inspection would involve breaking open decorative walls and removing the safe from the cement capturing it."

"Hum-m," Hickey mused, "and because that would be expensive and very disruptive to the wealthy property owners, it was never done?"

"Right, the safe was considered a liability and taken off the market. I'd even bet the owners have opted to abandon the installations for an alternative."

"I can't punch holes in that theory, Carver, anything else?"

"Yes. Touch base with Margo later on, see if she's established if someone put up the brooch that was in the safe as security for a loan, and don't hesitate to keep me informed."

Carver pulled into the old Taylor Building's underground parking, now properly illuminated after a fire department inspection. He drove past the fire-scarred areas and parked in his slot at the bottom.

The rejuvenated lighting, however, wasn't cause for him to let his guard down while on his way to the elevator.

His office was deserted when he arrived.

Feet propped up on the corner of his desk, he flipped through the Chicago Yellow Pages he'd taken from a wall of shelving.

The blurb that Titan Iron & Steel had created, attested to manufacturing everything from safes to battleships, not the rubber safes, but battleships in Chicago brought a question mark to Carver's face. The doubting frown left when it showed they owned a shipyard in Norfolk, Virginia.

He dialed the Chicago number and had the president, Mr. Granger on the line within a minute. He was ecstatic that Carver had hopes of solving a problem that had stumped them for years. No insurance company would accept liability on the Titan safe, once so highly regarded in the industry. Sales had dried up and unsold inventory was taking up space for no purpose.

After a short discussion Mr. Granger agreed to e-mail him a letter of confirmation that his company would pay twenty percent of the million-dollar surety bond placed on each installer. The technician who installed the safes in Los Angeles: William Wells. A six-foot-one Caucasian, now thirty-two years old, had quit his job five years ago after working almost five years for them without a blemish on his record. His picture and fingerprints would be included in the e-mail.

Within ten minutes of the call it arrived. On seeing the picture of Wells he almost fell from his chair. Although at the time he'd worn his hat brim turned down, he was almost positive that it was a picture of one of the bozos who'd used the woman hostage at Gino's Place and fled the scene.

Without a blemish indeed, this fellow had surely changed his spots. But that wasn't all that captured his interest in the guy. He had an odd feeling in his gut that he'd seen that face sometime in the distant past. Not from police records, but where, eluded him.

He sat at his desk for at least four minutes, searching his memory for the answer to his dilemma. He'd struck out, and decided he'd wasted enough time.

He left the office and drove the silver streak to a kiosk on Western Avenue, Gus Stanlosky's little corner of the world. A two-time loser turned straight, Gus peddled newspapers and magazines, cigs, cigar and candy bars to make ends meet. And he even shone shoes, if someone was desperate enough to sit on the cracked leather chair that was a relic from the past.

In things underworldish, Gus was a veritable encyclopedia, although no one but Carver had gotten him to share his valuable information. It happened that Carver was the sole possessor of evidence that could put old Mr. Stanlosky away for a lengthy time.

Carver tapped him on the shoulder to gain his attention, stepped up and sat on the elevated antique shoeshine chair. The legendary safecracker gone straight out of necessity, smiled at him and spoke his greeting in his unique tongue. As he had no teeth, hardly anyone understood him, and that was the way Gus wanted it.

"Can't help you, Mr. Frye," was his answer about the rash of unsolved domestic safe robberies a few years back. "Them jobs has me baffled, too."

"Scout's honor?"

"For sure, Mr. Frye. Best I can do is put out a few feelers."

When shown the picture of William Wells, Gus shook his head in the negative. "I ain't never seen that dude before."

Carver got down from the shine chair and pressed a fin into the outstretched palm. "Thanks anyway, Gus."

As he was about to pull away from the curb his cell pulsed. He plucked it from his belt and put it to his ear.

"It's me, Carver," said Margo's enchanting voice. "When I left the Bradley place shortly before noon, Lillian still hadn't heard from her sister. Also, I've checked with the people on the list most likely to own the caliber of brooch Lillian says isn't hers, nothing there. The inspector's had it appraised, its value is in the range of sixty-five thousand."

"That's interesting stuff, Margo. Anything else?"

"Yes, I talked with Steve Holgate about an hour ago. He says hello to you, that he's feeling much better and wants you to drop in if you have the time. By the way, how's your arm?"

"Coming along quite nicely, thanks. I've a lot on my plate, Margo, and I need you to locate a whorehouse, operating as the Pal Shirt Company somewhere near the docks in an old three-story mansion. The name isn't listed with the phone company."

"I'll get right on it, Carver. Take care now, and if the cast on your arm starts to itch, I'd suggest you get yourself a knitting needle."

He chuckled. "Can you see me buying a knitting needle? Bye for now, Margo."

Nearing two in the afternoon, he headed for *Dekker's* restaurant. He'd had a late breakfast with James Hickey, but when he felt he needed a break he could always talk himself into a snack. He needed something to calm the anxieties building at the thought of meeting up with Basil Upton at his health club.

Charles greeted him in the restaurant's entrance rotunda, and asked if he'd gotten Helen's invite for him and Margo for dinner, come Saturday.

"Yes, I have, Charles. But tell Helen that we won't be coming unless she served up my favorite."

"And what's that?" Charles asked.

"Cabbage rolls, as only she can make them."

Charles grinned. "Tell her yourself. She happens to be in the dining room pecking away at your favorite snack of Dungeness crab legs, my famous sauce and a glass of dry sherry."

"That's what I came by for, but I've only got a half hour, heavy duty stuff with Lillian Bradley." He walked into the dining room where it was mostly women chatting over tea, sounding like a flock of seagulls hovering over a shrimp boat unloading its catch.

Helen was seated alone, wearing a contented look that spelled out the fact her husband owned the place. After swirling a crab leg speared on a two-tined fork into a dish of her husband's famous sauce, she looked up. "Carver!," she exclaimed, as he came over and kissed her soundly on the cheek.

The chatter in the room waned as others looked on.

"How's my best gal?"

"Just fine, love."

He sat on the chair beside her and moved his left arm about to quell a cramp that had come up. Moments later, his dish of crab and glass of sherry arrived and between bites they were chatting up a storm.

"Good Lord, is that a cast I saw, barely peeking out from the sleeve of your jacket when you moved your left arm about for a moment there, Carver?"

"Yeah. It's nothing serious, just a hairline fracture."

"The wreck of your Jaguar in West Covina?"

"Yes."

"I wish you'd leave the solving of this arrow murder business to the police, Carver. You've always had more than you can handle since going out on your own. Why get involved?"

He smiled lamely at her. "I am the police, Helen. At least on a temporary basis. I was sworn in by Inspector Conroy, shortly after our friend Steve Holgate got shot."

Helen's eyebrows went to the top floor. "I'll be damned, if you aren't the most clothed-mouth son of a bitch God ever created."

He shrugged apathetically. "That's the way the ball bounces, Helen. There's been lots of surprises since I took on Morton Bradley as a client. But I'm quite certain this mess will be solved soon. The crud involved won't be long at being found out. Things are coming together faster than I expected."

Helen shook her head wondrously; "You are simply amazing, Carver Frye. It's no wonder your fees are the envy of your profession. I hope you're not working pro bono on this one, you could get yourself killed."

He swallowed the last morsel of crab and looked up. "Then it really wouldn't matter, would it?"

"You're damn right it would. We'd lose a good friend and Charles would be minus his best customer. You've already come close to pushing the envelope to the limit, how many more wrecked cars and broken bones does it take for you to realize that mortality doesn't come with nine lives?"

"Thanks for your concern, Helen. Anyway, I've got an appointment to meet." He got up from his chair, leaned down to kiss her on the forehead, and left the restaurant aware that the snack would appear on his statement at month end.

Chapter 17

CARVER parked beside Lillian Bradley's Mercedes convertible in the Health Club's lot and found her just sitting there looking straight ahead, as though in a trance.

He came up to her wearing a frown. "Hello, Mrs. Bradley." She looked his way as though spellbound and he tapped her lightly on the cheek.

"Oh, Mr. Frye, sorry, I was daydreaming."

He raised his eyebrows.

"Really. I'm worried sick about Beverly. I've called and called since she left me at the pool yesterday afternoon. And she didn't show up for our hair appointment today."

"Does she have a friend that would cause her to forget?"

"She has lots of friends, but she's never done this to me before. She'd always call if she couldn't meet a time we'd arranged. In this day and age when a phone fits in your pocket or purse, there's no excuse not to call. That's what has me worried."

"It's about twenty-six hours since she left you yesterday. The police won't act on a missing person report until after forty-eight hours. So, let's hope for the best and get on with why we are here."

She took hold of his arm and walked with him to the club's entrance. "I've never come in the front door before," she disclosed and pointed. "There's a side door near to the rear of the building that opens onto a hallway to his living quarters."

On entering the club's lobby he was impressed. The Straight Line Health Club was anything but mediocre. A marble-topped counter blended with the marble columns and flooring in a spacious, expensively furnished waiting area.

In back of the counter, tended by a muscle-bound female, doors led to the gymnasium, work out areas and change rooms. She looked their way and said, "Hello, may I help you?"

"We've come to speak with Mr. Upton," Carver responded.

"About what, joining the club?"

"It's a personal matter."

"I see, well, Mr. Upton is tied up at the moment and cannot be disturbed. Maybe if you came back in say, an hour or so?"

While she was talking a well-dressed young man came through the entrance doors and walked directly up to her. Overly impatient, he stated his reason for being there. "I've only got about ten minutes, Miss. I'm new in town, live nearby and have been told this is a good club. If you'll show me about and I like your facilities, I'd like to join."

Having already spent the commission she'd make for signing this young man to a contract, she gave him her full attention, and in doing so, summarily dismissed the couple she'd told to come back to talk with Mr. Upton.

"I'll be happy to show you around," she chimed. "Please, come with me."

The moment she disappeared with the prospective client through a door in back of the counter, Carver and

Lillian headed for a carpeted hallway to the rear of the building.

After indicating the door on the outside wall she'd mentioned earlier, she pointed to an inner door at the hall's end and said, "That's his private entrance. He parks in back, off the lane."

He held a finger to his lips as they approached the door to Upton's living quarters, and found it locked. "Would you like to know what's tied him up that he can't be disturbed?" he whispered.

"Yes," she anxiously responded.

Within only moments he'd picked the lock. As they moved silently along a carpeted hallway, she touched his sleeve and pointed. "His bedroom;" she mouthed silently.

"Let's have a look," he whispered. Very gently he turned the doorknob and opened the door wide.

Never having met Basil Upton, the first he saw of him was the top of his head facing the doorway. He was lying on his back, naked. Astride him, facing the open door was a naked red-head with a more than an amply-endowed upper respiratory section. She smiled at Carver in particular and said gleefully, "Get undressed you two, an' we'll make it a foursome."

"What the hell are you talking about?" Upton queried while his hands groped her breasts and saw that she was looking straight ahead.

His companion never lost a beat in her rhythmic motion, and smiled down at him. "We've a pretty classy looking couple standing in the doorway looking on, Basil. I'm inviting *him in,* and I'm sure you'll like playing with, *this good lookin' chick.*"

"Not bloody likely," Lillian exploded on bursting into the room.

In an instant Upton had discarded his playmate and was sitting on a side of the bed pulling a sheet about him. While he was occupied with this, Lillian Bradley slapped him hard on the cheek and spit in his face. "You son of a bitch, we're through!"

He stood and slapped her so hard, her newly fashioned coiffure fell apart. She landed on her back in a corner of the room, blood trickling from her mouth.

The next person he faced was Carver, who ducked under a straight right and threw one of his own.

As Upton fell to the floor, blood was spurting from a nose that had been flattened. He was out cold.

Carver confronted the naked bimbo on her hands and knees on the far side of the bed, with a big grin. "He's all yours, sweetheart. When he comes to, tell him I'll be back and will want a few questions answered. The name is Frye, by the way, Carver Frye."

He retrieved the disheveled and bleeding Lillian Bradley from the floor, and escorted her along the hall to find a bathroom. Its door was open and they went in. As he washed blood from her mouth and from his fist, using Kleenex tissue from a nearby box, he looked in the mirror above the sink to see an electric shaver hanging there.

The walls being reflected in the mirror, contained a profusion of pictures, most of which were pornographic. People caught in the act of exposing themselves to a degree that was totally vulgar.

"Oh! my goodness, let's get out of here," Lillian cried when she looked at the mass of pictures, "that man is a pervert. I had no idea what I was getting myself into, Mr. Frye."

Having admitted to being here twice before, he was sure she was putting on an act. "Well, you're clear of him now," he said and escorted her from the apartment.

They left the building by the door she'd used previously, which opened onto a narrow cement walkway leading to the alley.

A wall of closely planted cedars hid the walk from the parking lot, but for a slightly wider space between two trees that allowed one direct entry onto the customer parking area.

After establishing that she had settled down and was capable of driving, he looked on while she drove off.

Chapter 18

CLOSING in on thirty-nine hours since Steve Holgate was shot, Carver pulled into the hospital parking lot to visit with his friend. On stepping from the elevator onto the third floor, he observed Steve holding to the arm of Inspector Conroy.

While he stood at the open door to Steve's private room, they walked slowly along the hallway towards him.

"Howdy Steve, you're looking great," Carver chimed. "Margo informed me that you are able to have visitors." While they shook hands, Carver grinned at the inspector who simply returned the grin, aware that Carver really wasn't under his direction, but doing them a favor by taking on this case.

"I'm glad you could take the time to visit, Carver. How are things going with the investigation?" Steve asked.

Carver came up with a pained look. "You don't want to know, just get well and then we can talk about this rotten business."

When they'd entered his room and were seated, Steve got right to it. "I'm well enough to have my mind involved here, so give me a leg up on what's happening. How do we sit after forty hours of you agreeing to help out on this case?"

Anxious to have something to feed to the media, the inspector's interest heightened. "Yes, tell us, Carver. Give us something that's not already public knowledge. What's this about a left over brooch from Bradley's safe, that isn't the property of Mrs. Bradley? And I've only just learned that detective Hickey has pulled from the computer files, a list of items stolen in the Titan safe robberies of a few years back. What's that about? And we've just been informed by Lillian Bradley that her sister, Beverly Hughes, has been missing for about twenty four hours."

"You know a lot," Carver responded.

The inspector's expression was that of a youngster on the bench itching to get into the ball game, and he continued. "I was at Charles Dekker's restaurant for a very late lunch, today, and he told me that you'd told his wife that this mystery would be cleared up real soon. We need to know something that will satisfy the media, Carver. They are camped out at the precinct like a swarm of locust."

"From what I've just heard, you are as informed about this fiasco that's kept on growing, as I am. There's nothing I can add."

"That's absolute Bull."

"Scout's honor, Steve."

"Then why is Hickey wasting his time looking into the Titan safe mysteries of years ago? What good is the list of valuables that were missing?"

"Hell, I don't know why he wasted his time looking into that, but something useful did come of it. The brooch that Mrs. Bradley says isn't hers, doesn't match up with any that were stolen in the Titan safe fiasco of years back. So, let's give the guy credit, he's not spinning his wheels."

"So we got a plum from you, did we?"

"Call it what you want, Steve. Anyway, I'm happy to see that you're mending so quickly. But I have to run, my plate is full."

"That's one of your favorite expressions," Steve said, seemingly annoyed.

Carver got to his feet, reached out to shake his hand and left the two of them staring at one another like a couple of pros called out on strikes, on what should have been called balls.

Chapter 19

NOT having heard from Margo regards locating the Pal Shirt Company's whorehouse, he drove to the dock area in the hope of finding Padonti's messed-up club full of workmen cleaning up, allowing him to blend in without attracting attention.

Aware that his silver-gray Jaguar would attract attention in the area, he eased into a parking slot on a city right-of-way that dead-ended at the foreshore. Metal posts blocked all but foot traffic from using a dock that jutted a fair way out into the water. He walked the block from there, to Gino's Place.

The second and top floor of the building where Padonti's spacious office and separate living quarters were located, had a fantastic view of the Pacific that lapped endlessly at the cement retaining walls containing the fill on which the building had been constructed.

Workmen in the throws of cleaning up the massive room littered with broken and fire-charred chairs and tables, smashed glasses, beer bottles, cans and whatnot, were sorting the stuff into piles. The stench of stale beer and charred wood was next to overpowering.

"Is Padonti here?" he asked of a workman who eyed him closely as he came down the stairs while Carver was on his way up.

"Who wants to know?" challenged the big fellow carrying a garbage can, and stopped to block Carver's way. But when police credentials got flashed, Carver waited for his answer. "No. He ain't in. He took off half an hour ago an' won't be back 'til later tonight."

As though suffering from an acute attack of cramps, Carver grimaced and looked up in pain at the fellow. "That so, well, anyway, I desperately gotta use the bathroom in his office, is it locked?"

"Yeah, but I don't know if he'd like yuh usin' his can."

He took a step upward and faced the fellow. "Would you rather I pissed and crapped on the stairs? I ain't holdin' this much longer."

The guy made up his mind in a hurry. "All right, but I'll be waitin' on yuh." He returned to the landing at the top of the stairs, unlocked the office door, entered, ushered

Carver in by pointing to the can, sat on the arm of a leather chair nearby and called out, "Don't stink up the place."

Carver locked the door to a small cubicle that housed a toilet and sink, both badly discolored and chipped. A rack on the wall displayed a well-used hand towel. On the linoleum floor in a corner, was a cello-pack of toilet paper with one roll missing. He was in luck, very little of the roll on the dispenser had been used.

He removed the hollow plastic roller in which the manufacturer-installed deodorant had long since evaporated.

Depending on usage, it would be a day or so before his high-tech replacement roller would be discovered. He flushed the toilet a couple of times and left the room cinching up his belt. Coming abreast of the worker who appeared reluctant to put down a copy of 'Playboy' he heaved a sigh of relief. "That feels better," he said while the guy's attention was focused on the centerfold.

Without a word, the surly worker returned the magazine to a corner of Padonti's desk, went to the bathroom, opened the door and looked in. Returning to face Carver, he said, "You didn't stink up the place or crap on the floor, so I guess I won't have to clean nothin' up or mention to Gino that you was here."

"Suits me, I won't mention it either," Carver said, and left the building.

A half hour had passed since he'd parked. Concerned that a tire bomb could have been placed, he checked, got behind the wheel, backed out of the slot and was about to start away when his cell phone made itself known. He pulled to the side of the road to answer it. Margo's captivating voice was pure pleasure to his ears.

"It's taken me some time, Carver, but about an hour ago I finally located the shirt company. While I observed the place for a time, three of what I'd guess were call girls, arrived in taxis with their customers and went into an old mansion at 211 Signal Avenue, near the railroad tracks"

"Good work, Margo. Thanks."

"After the John's came out and got into their taxis, a short time later taxis arrived to pick up the same girls and drove off."

"Great work, Margo. Now that you're in the area, would you consider a hamburger take-out supper and keep an eye on the place? I'd like to know if this guy Basil Upton makes a visit there."

"Sure, I can do that for you. I'll phone mother and let her know I won't be home for supper. But I don't have any idea what this Basil Upton looks like."

"Look for a guy wearing a bandaged nose that got broken earlier this afternoon."

"Some of your work?"

"Good guess. Phone me if anything of interest rears its head. I'm expecting a call from detective Hickey, the beanpole you haven't yet met. And thanks again for finding the place Margo."

No sooner had he returned the phone to his belt, it alerted him again. "So how did it go with Upton?" was the immediate question thrown at him.

"I'll bring you up to speed on that later, James. Did you establish the location of those four Titan safes?"

"Yes, I did. My credentials impressed the hell out of the household staff, and I was shown around like royalty."

"How about giving me some facts instead of the details of your tour, James."

"Yes, well, like you predicted, the safes were embedded in concrete walls that are dressed in stonework on the outside. And ivy is growing on the outer walls leading up to the parapet walls of the balconies. After the unsolved Titan safe robberies of yesteryear, three of the four had the safe doors removed and the cavities used for artificial floral displays. They were quite striking."

"Are you something of an interior decorator, what about the other one?"

"Used simply for unimportant stuff, I was told. All the owners have installed floor safes from a different manufacturer."

"Good work. Hopefully, we'll find the time tonight when it's dark enough, to prove our point from just one of the balconies."

"Which one;"

"The one that's closest."

"That'll be the one the maid told me is being used for unimportant papers and such."

"Whatever, James. Margo has located the shirt company's whorehouse at 211 Signal Avenue. She is staking the place out until we arrive. Can you make it there say, about 7:30, you'll spot my wheels parked beyond the line of sight."

"Make it 7:45. I don't want a speeding ticket."

Carver chuckled. "Okay, see you when you get there. By then I'll have gotten the lowdown from Margo and sent her along home to check on her mother."

"Aren't you the lucky one."

"Is that so?"

"Yeah, you've got bird dogs doing your leg work; while you sit in the catbird seat calling the shots."

"Hickey, you're blowing my mind. I'm used to taking abuse from the governor, right on down to people like Steve Holgate, and even the women's auxiliary in charge of crippled water foul. So, keep your dumb ass thinking to yourself or I won't invite you for dinner at *Dekker's* after we pack it in for the night."

Hickey chuckled. "Guess I must have hit a nerve. I'll hang up now and be on my way."

While Carver was cruising about the area where the shirt company had its whorehouse, he spotted the tan-colored Ford Focus he'd rented for Margo while her car was being repaired. It was her car's roof he'd landed on during the underground parking garage fiasco.

She'd parked where she could keep an eye on the entrance of the old house situated on a lane corner.

"You must be weary after such a long day," he remarked on getting in beside her, "anything new?"

"Not a lot. I spotted a black Lincoln town car leaving the lane in back of the house. I don't know if it even stopped there as my view is blocked by the high wooden fence around back."

"Thanks again for finding this place, Margo. Detective Hickey will be along shortly and I'd suggest you call it a day. Say hello to your mom for me, and don't forget that come Saturday I'll be picking you up at seven for dinner at the Dekker residence."

She smiled his way. "Don't go taking any chances you don't have to, Carver. I'd like you all in one piece, too."

While closing her car door silently, she blew him a kiss. He willingly reciprocated before she drove off.

He returned to the silver bullet and let his mind wander in the euphoric feeling she unfailingly created when in her company. Should he not send her flowers too, like he had her mother? Was he being overly concerned that his past connection with the Los Angles Police Department would result in a like circumstance, as had happened with his father to leave his mother a grieving widow?

Two minutes before eight, Hickey parked behind him. "Don't ask," he said on opening the Jag's door to see Carver glancing at his watch. "Bloody traffic," Hickey fumed.

An insignificant sign with small black lettering, propped up on a front windowsill of an old three-tiered house, much like the one in the small town of Wilmette, Illinois, which Carver had grown up in, read simply: Pal Shirt Co.

They entered the rear yard through a poorly latched gate in the high fence, to find it overgrown with weeds and cluttered with junk. On a porch of weathered boards, a barrel tub, ablaze with a profusion of well-tended flowers, looked as out of place as a politician sitting in on a think tank.

They made their way to a back door that was locked. Peering in through the flimsily-curtained upper part of the door, Carver saw a lengthy linoleum-clad hallway that lead to the front door, which was also curtained.

He picked the lock, and when the door opened on well-oiled hinges he looked surprised. They went inside, closed the door and listened. Apart from the subdued sound of cool air rushing through the floor vents from the furnace below, it was silent as a tomb.

Having noticed a light go on in a third floor room at the front of the house while waiting for Hickey to arrive, Carver put a finger to his lips, they couldn't chance making any sounds.

While moving cautiously along the hallway towards the front door, they heard the muted voices of two males coming from above and stopped in their tracks. Even though the voices turned vituperative at times, neither he nor Hickey could make out what was being said.

Again they moved closer to the foyer and stairs to the upper reaches of the house, where the voices were much clearer. They listened intently.

Showing surprise, Carver turned to Hickey and whispered, "I'm sure one of those voices belongs to Basil Upton. I heard that high-pitched nasal intonation when I was in his bedroom this afternoon."

"You were in his bedroom?"

"Yeah, I'll tell you about it later."

They continued on to the stairwell, stopping from time to time when the hall flooring beneath the linoleum creaked.

At the front entrance, where the hall opened up into a foyer, the staircase to above looked to be in a poor state. Stripped of carpeting, the stair treads creaked when stepped on, and the many missing balusters that supported the hand railing, had undoubtedly rendered it unstable.

Avoiding the center of the staircase they made their way cautiously from landing to landing. On reaching the third floor, the unmistakable cry of a female came through loud and clear.

Seeing an enlightened expression on Carver's face turn into a cynical smile, Hickey whispered, "Do you recognize the voice?"

"I sure do, and so should you after taking her statement at the Bradley mansion. If that isn't Lillian Bradley's sister, Beverly Hughes, I'll eat dirt."

While the raised voices of Basil Upton and the other male intermingled with that of the terrified female, they moved cautiously on the creaking hardwood floor toward the door at the end of the hallway.

"Cut off more of her goddamned hair, Bill," Upton ranted.

Carver was hoping the one named *Bill,* would turn out to be William Wells, the technician who'd installed the Titan safes in the Los Angeles area.

"No!, No!, Please don't!" cried the terrified female. "I'm not lying to you Mr. Upton, I don't know anything about money you say is hidden in the Bradley mansion."

"Maybe the chick isn't lying Basil. In the last hour we've slapped her around like a rag doll, tied her to this chair and hacked off most of her hair."

"I don't agree, Bill. She's lying. Two sisters as close as that slut Lillian who screwed her way into marrying Bradley, and this part time model with a body that won't quit, surely must have wormed their way into Bradley's confidence one way or another."

"And you think there's something like a couple million stashed away?" queried the one called Bill.

"At the very least, two million, and you better believe it. The call girl part of his business was very lucrative, but just peanuts compared to what some fine upstanding Johns have paid out in blackmail over the years."

"Yeah, I guess maybe you're right. We ain't done too bad with our share along the way since I've been involved. But now that Gino's back, and Bradley's been snuffed out, he'll be coming to us for a larger piece of the action."

It turned quiet for a few moments. When the dialogue began again they crept closer to what looked like a door made of solid oak.

"So, how do you suggest we get this broad to open up, Basil?"

More silence, then a devilish chuckle. "I got my nuts off around three in the afternoon, before that son of a bitching Carver Frye busted into my bedroom."

"He the guy what broke your nose?"

"Yeah, a lucky punch. Anyway, I think this little dolly will open up if we strip her naked and put the blocks to her on the floor. We can take turns with her, if it comes to that. Yeah, she'll come to her senses and tell us what we want to know."

"Hell of an idea, Basil. We should'a thought of that sooner. What do you say, doll?"

"Please, mister!. Please don't do that, I've been telling you the truth. I don't know anything about hidden money. Please, mister!."

They read the fear in Beverly's cries and a moment later, heard what sounded like material being ripped.

Carver had heard enough. He went to the door and turned the knob cautiously. It was locked. As he pondered his next move the dialogue from the locked room continued.

"Wow. What a great looking set of tits you have, babe. And for your information the name of the guy who's gonna put the blocks to you first, is not Mister, it's William Wells."

On that note Carver reached for his Beretta, stood back and took a run at the door. It hardly budged, but a split second later shots rang out and splintered the wood perilously close to his head.

Not knowing where in the room Beverly Hughes was, he didn't return fire, but when he heard glass breaking he got off a burst of three shells at the door lock.

No sooner had he done so, and Hickey ran at the door with his shoulder, only to bounce back like a tennis ball.

After another burst from his .45, Carver opened the door with a well-aimed kick, rushed to a window now cleared of glass and saw William Wells running off through the well-treed property. He stopped, turned and fired at Carver in the window and took off again to disappear from view in the trees.

But to where, had Upton disappeared?

As Carver looked on, the answer came from the bottom of the fire escape ladder. A gun spoke twice, and the plaster ceiling above where Carver stood at the window showered him in white particles. He moved to one side and returned fire in the direction the shots had come from.

When no response came, he leaned out to see the guy hanging upside down. His ankle was trapped between the ladder's bottom rung and the wall of the house to which the ladder was attached.

He climbed down the wooden fire escape, dropped from about six feet up onto the lawn, kicked Upton's .45 away and ran in the direction Wells had taken in hopes of finding him wounded. He didn't want him dead. Alive, he was worth a fair chunk of money, courtesy of Titan Iron & Steel, in Chicago.

Wells had escaped. No trail of blood, nothing. He returned the Beretta to the holster under his arm, and went back to view Upton's predicament. His painful moans had now turned into intense shrieks of pain while blood dripped from his mouth.

With considerable effort, he lifted him from his entanglement with the ladder, aware that the leg and ankle were badly broken. The pain was so intense his cries were ear shattering as he was placed on the ground.

In the next moment he'd rolled into a ball on his side, hands holding to a gut that had taken slugs from Carver's gun and bleeding profusely.

"Are you okay, Carver?" Hickey called out from above.

"Yeah, I'm okay partner. How are things with Ms. Hughes?"

"She's a little the worse for wear, but I've got her calmed down and called for an ambulance."

"Good. And put in a call to the coroner's office while I see if Upton has any strength left to talk."

Upton didn't look good at all. A fractured nose was the least of his troubles. His leg lay grotesquely twisted as it jutted out at an odd angle from his curled-up body.

Carver sat alongside him on the ground, wishing he had something to lessen the fellow's pain. Beads of cold sweat had broken out on Upton's forehead while he moaned from constant agony.

Carver took a handkerchief from his pocket and wiped at the perspiration on his face. "Hold on there, Upton. An ambulance is on its way."

Eyes filled with pain and hatred while looking up at Carver, Upton got out painfully, in spurts, "An' so's the coroner. I heard you talking to your partner, an' know I'm a goner, Frye." He continued to grimace and spit up blood that drooled from his mouth to the ground. "So cut the bullshit an' light me a cigarette," he managed painfully, one word at a time while gritting his teeth from pain.

On reaching into Upton's jacket pocket, Carver was relieved to come out with a pack of Camels and a lighter. Had he to turn him from his present position to reach the other pocket to find what he sought, it would have been a test of will, even though he was a seasoned veteran at witnessing death.

He shook a Camel from its pouch, lit it and held it to Upton's quivering lips. It took a superhuman effort for him to suck the smoke into his lungs, and it was obvious his addiction to nicotine had come full circle.

For one who owned a health club and supposedly health oriented, it was a revelation of just how hooked a person could become on cigarettes.

"Feels good, but I know I'm not long for this world," Upton got out while grimacing in pain between words that had been coming in spurts since he'd been placed on the ground. And then, as if something humorous had crossed his mind, he managed a weak chuckle before he pieced together his next painful utterance: "We all die from something, you son of a bitch, Frye, but I'd just as soon it was a slow death from nicotine, instead of bullets from your gun."

Carver held the cigarette to his lips a number of times. He wanted to ask questions and learn what if anything a human in his situation would feel inclined to wash from his conscience, if indeed he had one and gained the strength to continue.

"You won't believe me, Frye," he continued, in spurts, "but I had nothing to do with the Bradley or Spencer murders. An' I didn't take no shot at the detective what used t'be your partner."

Hearing this painfully drawn out statement caused Carver's eyebrows to elevate. Upton had been his prime suspect from the beginning of this fiasco. Again he held the cigarette to his lips.

His mouth didn't open. Unseeing eyes and the expression on Upton's chalk-white face seemed to be mocking him, aware that he would be wondering whether or not he'd told the truth. After all, it was bullets from Carver's gun that had done him in. Why would a dying man, who's guts were leaking out onto the lawn, want to provide him answers?

While closing Upton's eyelids, he wondered if he was laughing on his way to wherever.

§§§§§§

After the ambulance and the coroner had left the scene, the police conducted an exhaustive search of the once great house of many rooms. They confiscated computers, cameras, video and DVD equipment, along with a record of the clients who'd frequented the shirt company's whorehouse.

They were various and sundry people from different walks of life, who'd been severely stung in the pocketbook for years. They'd been captured on film and DVD doing what comes naturally, but in contravention of their marriage vows.

The time spent by Carver and Hickey in exploring the unknown at 211 Signal Avenue had taken little more than an hour and a half.

The police were left in charge of things, but the detectives weren't finished for the night just yet, even though it was nearing nine-thirty.

Chapter 20

WHILE they were in the vicinity of Gino's club, Carver decided they should listen in on what if anything had been recorded in Padonti's office since he'd switched toilet paper rollers. They parked their cars at the now deserted right of way that dead-ended at the public dock.

After taking only a few steps in the club's direction, Carver placed earphones over his head and activated the transmitter. Instantly hearing voices and aware that Hickey was about to say something, he waved his hands like a traffic cop to forestall any intrusion.

Hickey got the message and waited expectantly. Carver removed the headpiece and looked wondrously at his partner. "How lucky can we get? It's like sitting in on a meeting that's in progress this very minute."

At precisely 9:46 P.M. Hickey picked the strip club's lock on the front door. On entering, they almost chocked from the overpowering stench of the place, aware that the ongoing job of clean up was only partly completed.

Guns drawn, they stood on the landing outside Padonti's office door as the muted voices within were being taped from the bathroom.

When Carver turned the doorknob to find it unlocked, they burst into the room so forcefully the door bounced back hard off an inner wall.

The rebound was blocked by Hickey, while their guns covered the four slack-jawed underworld types seated in the room. From complete surprise, their eyes were all but popping from their heads.

"Any of you creeps even move a muscle to touch the heat you're packing, you're dead meat. Now, which of you is called Big Tiny?" Carver said menacingly.

Seated at his desk, Chairman of the Board, Gino Padonti, his face ablaze with anger, stood and shouted. "Why you bust in ah here an' wanna know this, detective Frye?"

"Answer the question and point him out, fat head." Hickey directed as he stood backed against the door. "We have it on good authority that he's the creep who shot out the windshield and front tires of a Jaguar in West Covina. So, stand up and be counted, Big Tiny. You're looking at an irate survivor of your handiwork who's completely pissed off and looking to even the score."

The trio of visiting suits looked on in deep concern, as though trying to make up their minds over what action they should take. They were seated on chairs backed against a three-foot-high wall, above which a wall of windows offered a murky view of the darkening horizon and the Pacific Ocean.

The glass inside hadn't been cleaned of tobacco smoke for years. But Mother Nature frequently cleaned her side. Even now she'd sent a plume of water from the angry surf hitting the retaining wall thirty feet below. It lapped at the windows as Hickey looked on waiting for someone to make a wrong move.

Carver was also reading their thoughts as they stared him down. "Don't even consider it, fellows." His cynical smile warned of the consequences.

He went into the bathroom, shut the door, exchanged toilet paper rollers and returned.

For a time they may have thought he had weak kidneys. When he came out holding what the toilet paper roll holder had recorded and activated it; out came every incriminating word spoken in that room since their meeting started.

Looks of astonishment quickly turned into a show of deep concern. The incriminating dialogue although obtained without a judge's approval, which was unknown to them, had gained their full attention.

A suit of maybe thirty, the size of an NFL linebacker, who'd been one of the suits to take the hostage and flee the club, leapt to his feet and quickly reached for what Carver assumed was his gun from an underarm holster.

This move caused the Beretta in Carver's hand to speak with authority. The bullets drove the big fellow backwards through the glass, and created a spectacular display of glass shards that flew every which way.

Carver went quickly to where a window once stood and looked down. Blood was rising to the surface while the unobstructed view of the Pacific was as welcome as the fresh air invading the room.

The instant he'd fired at Big Tiny, Hickey's piece had also come to life and dropped the next punk who'd chosen to gamble. The gun he'd drawn hit the floor with a thud, as did his body.

"Anyone else want to get stupid?" Hickey challenged.

The visit to Padonti's office had now turned critical and Carver was on his cell phone to alert the harbor patrol. He wanted Big Tiny's body fished from the drink pronto, and hoped the gun the fool had attempted to draw would still be in its holster.

And maybe, if they got lucky, a slug from it would match up with at least one case in the pending or unsolved files.

While Hickey remained vigilant over Padonti and the remaining suit smart enough not to gamble, Carver searched the office as he'd done less than twenty-four hours earlier, in hopes of locating the rifle used to shoot Steve Holgate.

He emerged from a closet holding an AK-47 by its sling. If the bragging Big Tiny had recorded on tape for turning Carver's baby blue into a pile of junk was fact, his prints on the weapon and a bullet match would be a bonus.

He came over to Padonti seated behind his desk, and placed the automatic rifle in front of him. Wearing a look that warned the club owner not to play games, he leaned in close to face him. "Big Tiny worked for you, didn't he, Gino."

"No. No, Mr. Frye, he no work ah for me."

"Maybe part time he worked for you, is that it?"

"No. He's ah no work ah for ah me, ever. He just ah come here tonight with his ah friend."

"Which friend, the dummy on the floor my partner has phoned an ambulance for, or the jerk sitting there afraid to move because he's crapped his pants?"

Padonti remained silent while looking concerned.

"Is he the punk who took the woman hostage, and started blasting away as he left the club with Big Tiny, Gino?"

"No."

"What's his name?"

Gino turned cocky and flashed him a smirk. "Ask him."

In the next instant Carver yanked him out of his chair by his necktie and slapped his face repeatedly. "I asked *you* for his name, you creep."

In a high-pitched voice brought on by a tie that was choking him, Gino squeaked, "Peter Pan."

Carver smiled inwardly. He had to give Padonti full marks for having guts. He slapped him harder. "You will be the one from Never-Never Land, Padonti, This isn't a game, what's his name?"

"It '*is*' Peter Pan," called out the fellow whom Hickey was cuffing while reading him his rights.

Carver released his hold on Padonti's necktie and smiled facetiously. "I'll never again disbelieve what you tell me, Gino." He shoved him back onto his chair and searched his desk for a gun that could be construed as being in his possession. He came up empty and again faced Gino. "So the automatic rifle I took from your closet, belonged to Big Tiny, and you had him put it in there because—why? Speak up, I'll believe you."

"He's ah not ah too ah bright. Maybe, he don't understand the English. I tell ah my friend Peter Pan when he phone to tell ah me he's ah come over with a couple friends, not to bring guns. Big Tiny—he bring ah the gun. I tell him—put in ah the closet. Then we have meeting, eat some pizza, have ah some drinks an' shoot ah the bull."

"You tell a good story, and I suppose that's when you learn that this creep Big Tiny has been out gunning for me in West Covina. Well, stick with your story for now, it's a good one."

"It's ah the truth, Mr. Frye."

"Sure it is. What's the name of the fellow who was with Big Tiny the night your place got turned upside down and you spent the night in the slammer?"

Gino posed thoughtful a moment, looked up at Carver and shook his head in the negative. "I don't ah remember his name."

At that moment the staccato sound of a chopper overhead, along with the sound of sirens coming ever closer from the water and from the land, foreclosed any thought of continuing with Padonti.

As well, Carver's cell phone was asking to be answered. He flipped it open. "Yeah?" he hollered.

"Is this detective lieutenant, Carver Frye?"

"Sure is."

"This is Trevor Wilson the chopper pilot. Nice having you back on the force, Carver. Our search has located a body just below the surface and we'll have it retrieved shortly. Any instructions?"

"Hello there, Trevor" Carver shouted over the din. "This assignment is temporary, and should be over in a day or so at the most. And yes, I do have instructions. The fellow you fish from the pond probably has a weapon strapped under his arm. If that's the case, I'd like a rundown on it, pronto."

"We read, will keep you informed Carver. Over and out."

Carver turned back into the room to inform the police who'd arrived of the situation, and for them to take charge of Peter Pan and the guy Hickey had put a hole in, Garth Bencham, based on identification he was packing.

After the police and ambulance crew had left with their charges, Hickey looked somewhat mystified and turned to Carver. "How come you didn't book our friend, Gino? That smug look on his face is beginning to piss me off." He glanced at his watch, "its nine-fifty-nine," he groused, "how about we take on the food you promised to spring for at *Dekker's* restaurant?"

Carver glanced at Padonti and turned back to Hickey. "I believe Gino when he says the automatic rifle belongs to Big Tiny. So our fat friend here looks to be as clean as a well plucked duck."

Hickey shook his head in wonder of Carver's thought processes, gave him a sickly smile, dropped to his knees on the floor, held out his arms palms up and said in a voice emulating the dwarf who'd played *Tattoo, in Fantasy Island,* "*The foood, boss. The foood.*"

Carver burst out laughing at Hickey's antics before he turned back to Padonti. "I've a lot more questions, Gino. Give me your word that you'll be here all day tomorrow, and I won't put you in the slammer for the night."

"On what ah charge," Padonti ventured as Hickey got to his feet.

"Keeping dirty windows," Hickey injected; "you heard the offer. What's your answer?"

"I'll be here, Mr. Frye."

While approaching their vehicles on leaving Gino's Place, Carver said wearily, "It's been a long, hot and busy day, James. Maybe you'll want to shower and change before dinner, I sure do. Charles Dekker wouldn't let me in the front door of his restaurant, smelling the way I do."

"What time does his restaurant close?"

"Many times not until one or two in the morning. There's lots of late eaters in this town, and his bar, musicians and dance floor is another drawing card that keeps the kitchen open. I'll meet you there at eleven."

A news flash on the radio as Carver drove home, reported: *'Carver Frye, the celebrated private investigator, formerly with the L.A.P.D., temporarily attached to the homicide division in hopes of solving the arrow murders and the shooting of his ex-partner, detective Steve Holgate; hasn't been releasing anything on these arrow murders that would put the press in a feeding frenzy.*

However, we've just learned that in the last twenty-four hours he has hunted down and shot dead the individual who fired at and totaled his car in West Covina. Detective Frye and his partner James Hickey, were lucky to escape the wreck with their lives.

An unnamed source this reporter deems reliable, disclosed only moments ago that detective Frye indicated to him that the arrow murders would be solved in a matter of hours.'

Carver realized the hole he'd dug for himself in being so open with his friend the chopper pilot. He shouldn't have been so optimistic. Then again, he was satisfied with the manner in which the bits and pieces were coming together.

He parked the silver bullet on the street out front of his residence.

After quietly unlocking the door to his second floor suite, he looked cautiously about without turning on the hall lights, before he made for the master bedroom.

Stripped naked, he glanced longingly at his bed. Overcome with weariness he headed for the bathroom, wrapped a towel around the hard cast, turned on the shower and stepped in.

After steaming up the bathroom through neglecting to turn on the exhaust fan, he opened the door wide onto the bedroom to air out the room and clear the fogged-up mirror used for shaving.

After drying his body with a bath towel, he wrapped it around his waist and removed the one covering the cast on his arm.

The mirror now cleared of steam, he adjusted a wing of the mirror, plugged in the electric razor and shaved the left side of his face. He returned that mirror to the wall, positioned the other one and began to shave the right side of his face.

In the next instant, as though struck by lightning, the mirror and his image exploded into a million pieces.

His heart racing like a trip-hammer from shock, he dropped to his knees, looked up and saw an ugly hole in the mirror's plywood backing where his head had been.

Still in shock he looked himself over. No cuts. Taking the towel from about his waist, he used it to move aside shards of glass and crawled through to his bedroom, where he made his way along the carpet to the window wall. On looking up, he saw a neat hole in the glass that suggested a .270 bore rifle. He reached out and pulled the cord that would render the vertical blinds completely closed, aware that his habit of leaving them part way open had almost been his undoing.

He dressed for the street in fresh clothing.

Out front of the apartment block, he checked the new Jaguar for tire bombs, then changed his mind about driving the short distance to *Dekker's.* He'd walk there, and attempt to settle his nerves down.

At five past eleven, he entered his favorite eatery and found Hickey in the waiting area, perusing a wall of framed, glossy photos of celebrities and notables.

"See anyone you know?"

Hickey turned and looked at his watch. "You're late."

"Yeah, well, I have a legitimate excuse, James. Some piece of slime tried to snipe my head off, so I walked over here to settle my nerves down."

From the deep concern showing on Carver's face, Hickey realized this wasn't idle chatter. "Wow, that's not good. Where, did it happen?"

After listening attentively, Hickey was thunderstruck. "From here on, Carver, I'll bet your bedroom blinds will be properly closed. You, are lucky to be alive."

"That's for sure, James. Have you met my friend Charles Dekker since you've been here?"

"Yes. I told him when I came in that I was your partner, and you'd invited me for dinner at eleven. That was about half an hour ago. He offered me a seat in one of those overstuffed wing chairs, said he was very busy and disappeared."

While looking beyond Carver's shoulder, Hickey's face lit up and he said: "Here he comes now."

The instant Carver turned to acknowledge his friend, the restaurateur turned stark white and dropped like a stone to the marble floor.

After they'd attended to him, Carver sat him up on the floor. "Are you feeling okay now, Charles?"

"What happened?"

"When you saw me turn from talking with my partner, you passed out cold. What's with you? If I didn't know better, I'd think you were the one who tried to blow my head off little more than a half hour ago."

Still somewhat pale and unsteady as they got him to his feet, they sat with him until his color and breathing returned to normal. At this point, Charles looked very concerned and said disbelievingly; "Someone took a shot at you, Carver? That is devastating news. Thank the Lord you weren't killed." He smiled insipidly and said apologetically, "It's been very busy tonight, and I had to give out your table. But come along, we'll find one that's set up."

While they were seated, Charles asked as he stood at their table awaiting the arrival of a waiter, "Where did this happen, Carver."

"At my place. I was shaving, and as usual hadn't fully closed my Venetian blinds. The crud got my image in the mirror, and I dropped to the floor. Must have thought they'd nailed me and took off."

"Any idea who?"

"Yeah, you," Carver said in jest.

Dekker's face turned the color of chalk, and his words seemed to catch in his throat when he asked: "Why did you say that?"

He hadn't taken the jibe lightly, and this troubled Carver. "For God's sake, can't you take a rib? Tell me what you've learned about Bert Mustard."

"Bert Mustard?"

"Yes, the rich guy in the divorce case I've asked you and others to keep an eye out for. You left a message on my machine at the office, that you had some info about him. I've been far too busy to get back to you."

Charles reached for a glass of water from the table that had now been set up, and drained it in one continuous swallow. On returning the glass, he began running his thumbs around one another while his mind clicked fully on. "Bert Mustard came into the restaurant this afternoon, with a classy looking woman in tow. I overheard him invite her to a party aboard his yacht tomorrow night. Is that of any use to you?"

"Was she blond, brunette, what?"

"She was a tall red head, of about maybe twenty."

Carver chuckled. "He's till playing at being that age when he's fifty. Late yesterday afternoon he was dancing with a blond at the Bel Air Sands and invited her to his yacht. My shutter bug came up with nothing. But the right shot could cost Mr. Mustard a king's ransom."

"Maybe he was the guy who took the shot at you," Hickey ventured.

"That's what I was thinking," Charles echoed. "Has anyone besides Padonti whom you've put in the pen been released lately?"

"No. My best guess is one of his boys. I've been playing it pretty rough with them lately."

"That's some night you've had Carver. Your waiter will be along shortly. Oh, and bye the way, Helen isn't feeling well. She's asked me to extend her apology about having to cancel Saturday night's dinner with you and Margo."

Carver showed concern. "I'm sorry to hear that, Charles. Give her my love, and tell her to get well soon. Margo will be disappointed, but I'm sure she'll understand. And you had better see a doctor. Anyone who passes out like you did must have troubles. They may not show on the surface, but check it out, pal."

"I will, Carver. Nice meeting you, detective Hickey. Enjoy your dinners." He walked off as their waiter appeared.

§§§§§

"Thanks for the invite, Carver. That, was one hell of a meal," Hickey said while pushing his chair back to rub his stomach and smile his satisfaction. "So what's on our plate for tomorrow, besides checking out that nearby Titan safe we didn't have time for today?"

"You can check to learn if Big Tiny was packing a gun when he went for his final swim. If so, see how it fits in with our records."

"And…?"

"And line up a print man for tomorrow night. If that safe opens up from the balcony, I'll need his services for sure. And I'm almost certain we'll find Upton's prints and those of this guy William Wells on the snub nosed end of that safe if it opens up."

"What will that prove?"

"Hickey, your powers of reason are slipping. Think about it, If I couldn't reach to the back of Bradley's Titan safe with my long arms, how else would their prints get there?"

"I see you point, but I wish you'd let me in on your secrets. You must know something the rest of us don't or you wouldn't predict solving this mess in a matter of a day or so. Give me a bone I can throw into the mix, that will get the inspector off my back. They know for sure that you won't give them squat until you're good and ready."

"Right on." Carver signed the bill for their meal and got to his feet. "And don't betray my trust in you, James.

Anything leaks out, you'll think working with Steve Holgate was a piece of cake. And please don't call my private number before noon unless you are a death's door. Good night, James."

"Want me to drop you off at your condo?" Hickey asked on their way to the door.

"No thanks, I need to settle myself down after a rifle shot that almost took my head off."

Outside on the stoop, Hickey offered his hand and they shook. "Thanks again for dinner, Carver. And after what you've been through in the last day or so, I'd suggest you be very alert when you are walking home. I sure as hell can't solve this thing with you in your grave." He turned and waved as he made his way along the walk that would take him to the restaurant's parking lot.

While sauntering along the restaurant's sloping cement walkway, Carver reached the three steps down to the short lower level that led onto Sunset Boulevard.

He sat on the top step to relax in the warm night air, and took it deep into his lungs. Heavy clouds had blocked out the moon and the night was like the inside of a refrigerator as he watched Hickey's car drive off, its taillights becoming lost in a sea of red when he it turned onto the boulevard.

Seated there on the cool cement step, his thoughts dwelling on what he'd faced earlier this evening, he was aware that, had his chain been yanked, he'd have become just another taillight on his way out of a topsy-turvy world.

The closeness of the atmosphere caused him to remove his jacket while he pondered the idiocy of man's inhumanity to man. As he sat there, his thoughts were interrupted by a foursome of male revelers who'd staggered from *Dekker's* El Grande bar.

"You'll feel a hell uv'a lot bedder with some fresh air unner yer belt, Stuart," one of them bellowed as they came closer to where Carver was sitting.

He turned to observe the going's on, amazed that any of them could even walk. Looking like puppets on strings, one of them left the pack and stumbled willy-nilly along the walk in the direction of the street.

Coming abreast of Carver, he managed a supercilious grin before he staggered and spewed vomit over Carver's left shoulder.

As the stinking mess slithered down Carver's shirtsleeve, the drunk flipped forward and passed out onto his lap.

"Aw-w-w...shit!. Look what Stuart's gone an' done. Sorry 'bout that, fellah," said the Sherman tank in the group as he wove his way over. He picked his drunken friend from Carver's lap like a rag doll, and slung him effortlessly over his massive shoulders like a sack of wheat.

Completely disgusted, Carver looked daggers at the motley group, was about to give them a piece of his mind, but in the next breath decided that he'd had enough trouble for one night.

The C-note that landed in his lap as he sat there steaming mad and smelling like a garbage can, didn't alter his mood one iota, as he listened to what was in their inebriated minds while they staggered off.

"Ain't Stuart's fault," spouted one of them. "What the hell's the guy sittin' on them cement stairs for anyways? Yuh gets piles from sittin' on cement. He deserves t'get puked on."

"Yeah," another agreed. "An' what the hell did juh give him the hunnerd for, Andy? Probably juss piss it away on booze. I should go back, kick the livin' shit outa the guy an' get yer money back."

Their illogical banter faded away as they reached the boulevard. A car door slammed. A motor started, and a squeal of rubber accompanied their exit from his life.

Thursday-June 19

Chapter 21

ALTHOUGH he'd cleaned up the vomit as best he could with a handkerchief, some of it had slithered from his shoulder in the direction of the holster containing his gun. While sitting there steaming mad, he considered returning to the restaurant to clean up properly, but when a light breeze came up and the stench wafted away somewhat, he decided he would persevere until he got home.

He got to his feet and put on the blazer, relieved to find that it at least partially obscured the stench.

As he walked on along the boulevard, he realized that home didn't sit too well with his frame of mind at the moment. It was a place with an neat hole in a bedroom window, glass was scattered about the floor in slivers that only a vacuum could pick up. And there was a wing-mirror in his bathroom, downgraded to a piece of plywood now sporting an ugly, splintered hole that looked like an Andy Warhol painting. Soiled clothes were strewn about his bedroom floor, and no cuddly-soft female to replace the sheep he'd been counting for too long. Hell, maybe it was time he gave some serious thought to romancing Margo as a partner, in more ways than one.

He nurtured this last thought fervently for a time, before he found his mind working on this case he'd agreed to take on. After a time he realized he'd walked on much further than he'd intended, and now he had an uneasy feeling that someone had been trailing him a far distance behind.

When he'd look back to find no one there, it was unnerving. Was his mind walking a tightrope associated with paranoia? Or was it the heat of the black, moonless night that was adding to his preoccupation with life in general? He glanced at his watch, a half hour past midnight. He walked on.

So deep were his thoughts about the puzzling case he'd agreed to work on, he wasn't aware of anyone's presence.

As he was about to pass a dead-end cobblestone alley, a long-bladed knife slashed deeply into the area of his right shoulder. Instant pain shocked him to the reality of NOW!

A severe flow of blood was running down his arm as he spun about to face his attackers. There were two of them, big like trees, wearing head masks and dressed in dark clothing. They snickered menacingly while they deftly backed him into the alley, the trusts from their long knives coming ever closer.

Wincing from the excruciating pain in his shoulder, he reached for his gun and fired.

Dead silence. His gun had jammed!

His attackers chuckled almost gleefully as they made thrust after thrust while backing him deeper and deeper into the alley.

The blood leaking down his right arm had saturated the sleeve of his jacket and was running towards the back of his hand. He glanced down, aware that the blood hadn't yet reached the useless gun in his hand, and in the next instant he'd side-armed his Beretta at the fellow nearest him.

It hit the guy in the head and he cried out before he fell to the ground, silent.

"Nice arm, Frye," was the remaining attacker's remark as he came at Carver with a vengeance and spouted: "You ain't gonna make it, you crud. You ain't Houdini, so you can kiss your ass goodbye."

Again and again Carver got nicked—the next time, very painfully on his right arm which saw more blood appear on his jacket.

He was being moved backward continuously, and found that he'd been forced against the brick wall of a warehouse building.

"What yuh gonna do now, big boy? Whew-w-w-w, you stink to high Heaven, but that ain't were you're going."

Carver didn't respond. He was fully occupied attempting to elude the long-bladed knife while groping his way along the brick wall. He got cut again, and again. His jacket was now a mass of slashes with blood seeping through.

He came upon a doorway indentation, and quickly moved to the other side. He couldn't afford to be trapped in a confined space with this fellow who appeared to be simply toying with him.

On the other side of the doorway opening, he banged into a metal garbage can and felt for the lid, only to learn the handle was missing. He took it from the can and winged it like a Frisbee at his attacker. The guy ducked, and in those few precious moments Carver reached into the garbage can and came out holding a long-necked wine bottle. He wiped a blood-soaked hand on his trousers, grasped the neck of the bottle tightly and broke off its bottom against a metal railing.

"Nifty move, big nose," his assailant mouthed and laughed heinously. "But a bottle ain't no match for this sticker. Like I said, you—ain't gonna make it."

The loss of so much blood was causing the strength to ebb from Carver's body. In a super-human effort he avoided the next thrust, parried with the jagged bottle and could hear the knife wielder's jacket tear. He snickered and said, "Being as you're so confident, you piece of crap, who is it that you and your friend are working for?"

Another chuckle came his way, along with another knife thrust and again he felt more pain.

"I don't mind telling you that big nose, because you won't be alive in a couple'a minutes. We could have plugged you full of lead from the start, but that would have been too easy. Gino wanted you to suffer, and is paying twenty-five grand to see your pelt laid out cold from the cold steel of a knife. The guy you flattened with your gun to his head, goofed. He was supposed to get you in the shoulder much deeper than he did, to the point you couldn't use the gun we know you always pack. And if by some miracle you come out on top in this contest, we've got that covered, too. There's a surprise waiting for you at the head of this dead end alley, to even the score."

"It seems you've covered all the bases."

"Yuh got that right." His attacker chuckled and made another lunge.

Carver avoided that one, anticipated the next move and held up his left arm to ward off the blade's downward slash. It hit full force on the hard plaster cast under his coat sleeve. The knife left the guy's hand and became airborne. In those few precious moments while his attacker's astonished eyes traced the arc of the knife, Carver buried the jagged end of the wine bottle deep into his gut, and twisted. A horrendous, elongated, pain-filled cry split the night air. Summoning his remaining strength, for good measure he repeated the process twice more while the cries of agony continued like thunderclaps.

"Everything okay in there?" the backup at the mouth of the alley called out.

"Yeah," Carver managed weakly, while he searched frantically about the cobblestones in the darkness for his gun. He stumbled over the guy he'd hit with it, and cuffed him while the creep lay face down.

As luck would have it, the moon burst through the ink above and illuminated the blind alley like a searchlight. He spotted his gun, picked it up and fired at the guy who a moment too late realized he was facing trouble.

The Beretta didn't misfire this time, and hosed the fellow who'd come out of hiding with five slugs, which caused a reflex action that instantly triggered the guy's automatic weapon. This saw the cobblestones create a series of Roman candles before his dying finger left the trigger and he fell to the ground.

At this point, Carver was bleeding worse than a loser in the market crash of '87, but he was thankful to hear what he figured were police sirens coming closer.

At the throat of the narrow alley, a black and white pulled to a screeching stop, its headlights flooding the confined warehouse building area, to the point it looked like a night shoot for a movie.

Uniformed cops appeared from behind both doors that were flung open to act as cover, their weapons drawn and aimed at him.

He bowed down on his knees as if to Allah, and raised his hands into the air. "Don't shoot," he gasped in a pain-filled cry.

"I'll be damned," an officer blurted, "that's *Carver Frye!*"

"It sure as hell is," said his partner. "What's going on here, Carver? We were only a block away when we got a call that someone phoned saying there was a knife fight going on over here, and then we heard shooting."

While a short rundown was ongoing by a bloodied and weary Carver Frye, an officer radioed for an ambulance.

Although his strength was all but completely spent and he was bleeding profusely, Carver returned to the fellow he'd cuffed, turned him over and removed the black woolen mask. The guy was awake, and blood was leaking from a deep gash near his temple, where Carver's Beretta had struck him.

He smiled weakly down at the guy and took from an inner pocket of his jacket the picture he'd secured over the internet from Titan Iron & Steel. He made the comparison and said in a pain-filled voice, "I'm very pleased to meet you, Mr. William Wells. You and I will be having a serious discussion after I get patched up and catch up on some sleep." He staggered back a few steps to the officers and said, moments before he passed out, "Read him his rights and book him."

Chapter 22

WEARING a concerned look while standing alongside a hospital bed, detective Steve Holgate observed his ex-partner opening his eyes.

"So, you finally decided to check in here, did you?"

When Carver held to his look and smiled, the concern on Steve's face was replaced with one of relief.

Carver managed a weak chuckle. "Guess maybe I didn't have a choice, Steve. The last thing I remember was lying on a stretcher in an ambulance. How are you feeling?"

"A lot better than how you look. And I don't for a minute believe what I hear on the newscasts and read in the papers. No, my boy—the seventy-two hours you allow to solve a murder or write it off as a lost cause, doesn't really hold in this case."

"Is that so?" Carver sat up, squirmed his legs from under the covers to over a side of the bed, to find that he was wearing hospital garb.

At that moment a nurse entered the room to see him sitting up. Wearing a look of surprise, she stopped in her tracks. "Oh, so you're awake, Mr. Frye."

"Yes, and where are my clothes, nurse?"

"They are in the closet right there." She pointed and came over to the bed. "But they are not the items you were wearing when you arrived on our doorstep last night."

Steve chuckled. "That's because I was alerted that they were bringing you in. I was told you smelled like a sewer rat when they brought you to emergency. So I phoned Margo early this morning, and asked her to bring over a complete change of clothes from the wardrobe you keep at the office."

"That was good of her."

"Yeah, why don't you marry the girl? You need mothering, my boy."

Carver smiled. "I've given it some thought." He looked himself over to learn that he'd become the recipient of much in the way of bandages on his right arm and shoulder. And he saw that the left arm had also been looked to. "Hmmm, it appears I've been well looked after. But where is my gun and the contents of my pockets?"

"Why? Do you think you're going somewhere?"

"Believe it, Steve." He got off the bed and went to the closet as the nurse looked on dumbfounded.

Margo hadn't forgotten anything, including undergarments and shoes. He dressed while they looked on in silence, went to the nightstand beside his bed and recovered his wristwatch, wallet, phone and the gun that has almost done him in. "Where's the rest of the stuff?" he asked on turning to Steve.

"Right here in this envelope. interesting stuff—the picture of a guy named William Wells, and a copy of his fingerprints from the files of Titan Iron & Steel, no less. What gives with this, Carver?"

"What gives is nothing my friend." He reached out and took possession of the envelope.

"So why the big interest in this guy?"

"No interest, I simply want things returned to my files."

"You're lying."

"That so? Anyway, I'm happy to see that you are almost back to your miserable self again. It's Thursday, almost one-thirty in the afternoon, sixty hours since you got shot." He studied Steve for a few moments and looked bewildered. "They let you up and about on your own, so soon?"

"Yeah, I'm like you and the NHL players who get cut, stitched, and back onto the ice pronto."

"Anyway, Steve, will you be a good fellow and keep your nose out of this mess for at least the seventy-two hours?"

Steve shrugged his shoulders. "Okay," he readily agreed.

Carver made his way to the door, and out In the hall he took the *cell phone* from his pocket to touch base with Hickey; that he wanted to be picked up.

Chapter 23

"**YOU**, are one tough private eye," Hickey blurted when Carver got into his unmarked car. "I thought you were walking home last night after dinner; but no—you take a walk along what was probably a well-defined route and get yourself tagged with a knife. Maybe it's time you altered your predictability factor. What happened?"

"Cut the lecture, James. And you're right, but at the moment I'm not in the mood to discuss my habits. What's happening with the loose ends surrounding this conundrum, anything I should know about?"

"Yeah, when Big Tiny was fished from the water, a gun was still in its holster. Ballistics has matched it to the slug taken from the gas bar attendant's body, the serial numbers match with records kept by Trident Fuels, the gas bar operators. And the AK-47 you took from the closet in Padonti's office was the gun used by Big Tiny to send us into that gully in West Covina."

"That's interesting stuff. And the State of California has saved a bundle from the way that creep ended up. Swift justice. If he'd got to his gun before I got to him, he could have wasted both of us."

"Yeah, but tell me what happened last night. I was really surprised when I learned this morning that you'd bagged the guy in the picture emailed you from Titan in Chicago."

Carver smiled inwardly. "William Wells was the beneficiary of my early skills at chucking a baseball. When my gun jammed, I winged it at his head and laid him out cold. How's the guy who took the jagged wine bottle in the gut? He should be hurting real bad."

"He's dead. The I.D. he was packing shows him as Samuel Bondard, the guy I shot and gave a flesh wound in the leg in Gino's office."

"So he died, huh. Better him than me. Before he got careless, he bragged that Padonti was paying twenty-five grand to see me cut to pieces with a knife. Anyway,

James, let's get to this fellow William Wells and see what we can come up with."

The interrogations room at the 32nd precinct saw Wells sitting in the same chair Gino had vacated. As they observed him from the one-way glass, his expression was all ice. He was tall, had a muscular body, and but for a mustache was cleanly shaved. A bandage showed near his left temple where he'd been clobbered by Carver's gun. This six-foot-two individual looked so calm and collected, he could have been in a restaurant waiting to be served.

"Well now, we meet again, Mr. Wells," Carver remarked as he sat across the table to face him. "You will be doing time for the attempted murder of a police officer. Just how much of it, depends on your cooperation."

He turned and spoke to Hickey standing nearby. "Does a twenty-five year stretch sound about right to you, detective?"

"It sure does, and with no chance for parole."

Carver got up to move about the room, a cat toying with a mouse with nowhere to run and hide. "Matter of fact," he said on returning to the table, "you will be doing much more time than that. There's also the abduction of Beverly Hughes. Before he died, Basil Upton implicated you in that regard."

"Bull shit." Wells spat.

"Whatever, and your partner in the alley last night, a Sam Bondard, implicated Gino Padonti as the one who hired both of you to kill me. Also, we have it from a number of the girls operating out of the house on Signal Avenue, that you are one of their pimps. But that's nothing compared to them fingering you and Upton for being involved in the blackmailing of selected Johns, video taped and on DVD's, showing extramarital sexual encounters."

After a short silence in which the pending charges appeared to be registering on Wells, the door to the room opened. A uniformed officer entered and handed Carver a note.

After reading it, he turned to Wells wearing a look of total disgust. "There's more, Mr. Wells." He tapped the note with a finger. "This is confirmation that your fingerprints were on a note wrapped around a set of keys in the pocket of a gas bar attendant, whom you and Big Tiny robbed and murdered. And there's the bomb you placed that blew up my Jaguar and cremated a hard working tanker driver. He had a loving wife and two children."

The look on Wells' face had now changed to one of despair and he said, "So, what's in this cooperation bit you mentioned earlier?"

Carver didn't answer. He left the room with Hickey to let the creep sweat it out, if he had a conscience…

The instant the door to Steve Holgate's office banged shut, Hickey confronted his superior. "He's one of the guys who took those women hostage the night Padonti's club became a shambles."

"I'm aware of that, after seeing the email picture and wondering where I'd seen him before. There was so much happening in that short space of time, and them with their hat brims turned low, I didn't really get a look that fully registered."

"Why didn't you get into the safe tampering item? He sure as hell can't deny it. He was the only installer in this area."

"First things first detective Hickey. We need solid proof of his involvement. The prints taken from inside the bull nosed end of the Bradley safe were smudged and inconclusive. We require irrefutable evidence, and hope to secure that from prints taken from just one of the safe's we'll be looking at tonight. We'll start with the one being used to store items of no particular value. If we find what we're looking for, we can eliminate wasting time on the others."

"That'll be the old fellow whose wife is uglier than a pelican swallowing a fish. She's in the hospital at the moment with a liver ailment, a drinking problem."

"Well now, you sure have done your homework."

"Not really. I got that info from the attractive maid who answered the door and let me in while the owner was away on business."

"That bit about the pelican, too? "

"Yep."

Carver's phone pulsed. The melodious voice of Margo had a soothing effect on him and it showed: "Oh, you're alive, the last time I saw you was in a hospital bed, sleeping like a baby. I've been worried about you Carver. Is there anything I can do, anything you need?"

"Matter of fact there is, Margo. There's a key to my place in the top drawer of my office desk. It's on a ring with six that look identical. However, one of them has a very fine nick filed on the rounded end."

"Clever, boy."

"Anyway, if you'd be good enough to call up a maid service, you could let them in to clean up the place. There's broken mirror shards in my bathroom and some in the carpet of my bedroom below the window with a hole in it. There's, soiled clothes, and I haven't had time to dust, vacuum, wash the sinks and tub, send my laundry to the cleaners or straighten up the place. Will you look after that for me, please?"

She chuckled. "It sounds to me, like you need a full-time maid, Carver. I'd like to apply, and be first in line."

He sent her a kiss over the phone. "No application needed, Margo, and you're already first in line. Thanks, I'll talk with you later." He hung up smiling and turned to Hickey. "My car is parked out front of where I live. I need a lift to pick it up."

"Where are you off to?"

"Where I can relax, the Bel Air Sands."

"And what have you got for me while we wait for darkness to check out the safe at the pelican's residence?"

"Not a lot. It seems that you've recovered from you slight concussion, so find Padonti at his club where he promised to be. Read him his rights, and arrest him for the attempted murder of yours truly."

"That will be a pleasure."

"And if Wells plays ball by signing a statement of Gino's complicity in the matter, then the game is over for that fat little creep for many years to come."

After spending an hour or so on his cell phone while in his room at the Bel Air Sands Hotel, looking after business that required dovetailing into his busy schedule, he crashed on the bed and fell asleep.

He awoke to the cell phone's vibration, rubbed his eyes open and looked at the time: 7:30 P.M. He'd slept about five hours. With the sun still streaming through the window, he yawned awake and answered the call. "What's up, James?"

"I've got Padonti in a cell at the precinct, and a fingerprint technician lined up for tonight."

"All right then, I'll meet you at the pelican's nest at ten-thirty."

Hickey said "Okay," chuckled and hung up.

Carver continued a self-induced respite at the hotel, and turned on the TV for the first time since the arrow murder fiasco began.

Sure enough, stale news from a couple of days ago was still being hashed and rehashed, complete with pictures and interviews with no-name experts.

Opinions of how the murders took place in a locked room, ran rampant from both ends of the spectrum. There was even the suggestion that maybe a magician was involved. At that, Carver chuckled, turned the set off and lay back to continue resting his weary bones.

When he arrived at what was now referred to as the Pelican's Nest in prestigious Bel Air, he parked on the street behind Hickey's Chevrolet, got out and shook hands with Randy Stover, the fingerprint technician waiting there with Hickey, who looked at his watch and commented flippantly, "You're on time Carver, and Randy thanks you for that. He has a date with his girlfriend, so let's get with it."

Carver moved aside ivy foliage clinging to the stone-faced wall, above which was a balcony. He exposed the sturdy latticework the ivy had clung to for years.

After cautiously repeating the step by step upward process to secure a footing on the rungs, he reached the decorative cement railing, stepped from it onto the balcony and motioned for Randy Stover to follow.

The study drapes were tightly closed and music was playing softly within the room as Carver attempted to locate the trigger stone, while the fingerprint technician looked on.

In only moments he wasn't astounded, but the print man was, on observing the hinged back of the sixteen-inch diameter safe open up silently, attached to a large flat stone that formed an integral component of the multi-stone embedded wall.

Carver looked into the safe, saw that it was open at the other end and could hardly contain himself from chuckling.

The gentleman who'd been away on business, was fully involved at making passionate love to a woman on a leather couch.

And while Carver was being titillated, he spotted a box of prophylactics near to the front of the safe. He quickly turned about to stand backed against the opening to block out the sound of street traffic. He surely didn't want to alert the lovers as to what was happening outside their fish bowl, while Randy Stover did his thing on the inside of the bull nosed metal casing attached to the stone that had swung outward.

Alongside their cars on the street again, Carver began to chuckle before breaking into subdued laughter as the others looked on.

Taken aback at this, Hickey asked, "What's gotten into you, Carver?"

Through tears of mirth, he told them of what he'd seen. "Did she have red hair?"

"Yeah, flaming red hair, James. A fantastic body, and moves that I suspect would win prizes. You should have seen the show, it was awesome."

Hickey stood back shaking his head. "Wouldn't you know it? That was the maid he was involved with. No wonder she was bad mouthing his wife to me."

By eleven-thirty that evening the fingerprints of Basil Upton and William Wells had been matched to those found on the inside of the bull nosed Titan safe.

After Randy had left to meet his date, Carver suggested Hickey should head along home and get some shuteye.

"And what about you?" Hickey queried. "Let me guess, you're going down to cells and have a little talk with our Mr. William Wells."

"You're either a mind reader or an astute judge of character, James. Matter of fact, you and Margo have been so helpful, I'll be cutting you both in for ten percent each of what Titan will be paying out. The insurance company will be shelling out pronto, once I get William Wells' signature, admitting to his guilt of safe tampering."

Faced with the evidence, Wells was a willing signatory to admitting his guilt as the mastermind behind the altered safes. He also put in writing that Padonti had instigated the attempted murder of Carver, and signed a statement to this effect.

Wells was a sleaze ball who'd be putting in time behind bars for the first time in his life, lots of time. This would also be the dilemma of Gino Padonti who, once again would find his life draining away from behind cold steel.

Were they better off than those who didn't make it? Big Tiny, who'd been fished out of the ocean cold as a mackerel? Basil Upton, who'd met his waterloo full of lead and a broken leg while hanging upside down on a ladder? Samuel Bondard, reamed out with a broken wine bottle, who thought earning his half of twenty-five grand for killing a detective, was easier to come by than working for a living at a legitimate job?

These thoughts ran amok in Carver's mind as he returned Wells to his cell an hour after Hickey had left for home.

Having had a few hours of sleep before dinner at the Bel Air Sands hotel, and a short rest after; Carver returned to his silver bullet and drove from the 32nd Precinct parking lot with the top down.

The relaxing stereo music was as welcome as a woman's fingers through his hair. His mind totally at rest and in limbo, he drove where his subconscious was taking him and wasn't surprised to find that he'd parked in Basil Upton's spot off the lane behind the health club.

Something called instinctive intuition had been tugging at his mind, and had required nurturing, for him to be here. He walked along the narrow sidewalk to the side entrance door and picked the lock.

At the door to Upton's suite, he revisited the task, opened the door, went in and closed it.

Seated in a leather chair in the dead man's living room, he wondered what he was doing here, why had he come? Upon resting his right cheek on the palm of his hand, he was alerted to the fact that concerns for his safety and the myriad of loose ends associated with the arrow murders, had overtaken him completely. After his mirror had exploded, he'd neglected to finish his shave.

He hadn't been properly shaven while having dinner with Hickey at Dekker's, not while in the hospital or at the Bel Air Sands.

He got up and went to Upton's spacious bathroom, where he recalled seeing an electric shaver hanging from its cord by the mirror over the sink. He turned on the light, and there it was.

All the while he was shaving, the walls he'd seen only briefly in the mirror's background while wiping blood from the face of Beverly Hughes, were triggering his subconscious.

He frowned knowingly, abandoned the shave and began to look seriously at that which he hadn't paid full attention to before.

He assumed that some two hundred pictures were on those walls, showing hookers and others snapped in the act of being themselves and seemingly enjoying it. He was disgusted, but something within told him to keep looking.

After perusing some fifty pictures, he came across one of Lillian Bradley. She'd changed considerably since the time of the picture. He supposed this was Morton Bradley's doing, but in the long run he couldn't change what was inside, and this was the reason for his call to Carver, Monday morning.

After another fifty or so pictures, he was stopped cold in his tracks and stared intently at the photo. A redhead stared back at him, an unusual dye job for a woman of color. His best guess was that the photo had been taken about five or six years ago. It was her, sure enough— Helen Dekker.

Before she'd married Charles, she'd been a common whore. This in itself wasn't shocking, lots of broads who curried their favors for money, ended up as respectable married women, their skeletons carefully locked in the closets of their minds.

The real shocker was Charles, his reaction when Carver turned from talking with Hickey. His fainting and nervous demeanor was now cause to suspect that it was indeed Charles who'd been the shooter. He must have thought he'd hit his target when Carver dropped from sight to his bathroom floor. Seeing him alive in his establishment a short time later, had been too much of a shock to his system.

Good God—but why Dekker? Why? Then he put it all together. Morton Bradley, alias John Harvey, had learned that one of his hookers had married a guy with money. He was blackmailing her husband. This would work perfectly. There was a sizable age difference and Dekker worshipped the ground Helen walked on, which Bradley knew of.

While he looked at the picture, he was convinced that Charles Dekker had been paying blackmail to keep his young wife from learning that he knew of her sordid past.

If she learned that he knew of her life as a hooker, it would, quite definitely to Carver's mind, have caused a breakup of their marriage. It would be initiated by Helen. She was the proud one, too ashamed to face him.

His course of action against someone who'd been his friend and his boss at one time, was going to be distasteful. But he was convinced that, *his friend had actually attempted to kill him.*

Had Charles not taken things to that extreme he might have considered dropping the case and let it rot in the unsolved files. Still, that wasn't necessarily so, there was Steve Holgate. Put a bone in his teeth and he'd keep on gnawing away.

He returned to Upton's living room to turn things over in a mind where all the circuits were now connecting.

A hazy picture of William Wells popped up in a group shot he'd seen in Helen Dekker's photo album. He remembered being over to Dekker's house one night some four years ago, and recalled that he'd gotten pleasantly sloshed on Jamaican rum. At the time of the picture, Wells wore a full unkempt beard on his face and hippy-type long hair.

He now realized what had been bugging him when the guy's picture had come to him from Titan in Chicago.

Still in a quandary about a number of items, he returned to Upton's bathroom.

Among the last of the photos he came across was a group shot of William Wells, Helen Dekker and Basil Upton. It had been taken maybe six years ago, on a well treed boulevard in front of a large, stately-looking house with a roof-covered wrap around porch. Wells was planting a kiss on Helen's smiling face.

In the picture's background was a segment of a white dome Carver instantly recognized: the architecturally unique, Baha'i Faith Temple, in Wilmette, the town where he'd grown up.

The wheels of his mind were now spinning out of control. The possibilities associated with the picture's location required a follow up.

Now almost 1:00 A.M. Friday morning, he headed for home aware that his 72 hour time frame to solve the mystery had been eaten up.

Friday-June 20

Chapter 24

HIS mind alert to what he'd unearthed, he'd endured a night full of frustration, sleep hadn't come easily.

In the morning he made coffee from a jar tied to a commercial that touted it as being: *'as good as fresh brewed.'*

A little after nine Chicago time, he reached Titan's president. This fellow took his job seriously and wanted to be kept informed. He was elated at the outcome of an investigation that would reinstate the Titan safe to worldwide markets. One of his staff would phone shortly, to supply him with the further information Carver required about William Wells.

Prior to Wells being transferred by Titan to California, he had lived with his mother in Wilmette.

He phoned the number supplied him.

A pleasant sounding woman answered.

"My name is Clarence Trent, Mrs. Wells," Carver lied. "I'm with the phone company conducting a survey on long distance calls. Might I have a few minutes of your time?"

"Sure, Mr. Trent, I don't go for bridge lessons for another hour, and that's just across the street at Martha's house."

"Thank you, and how are the lessons going?"

He shouldn't have asked. Mrs. Wells was a talker. He got the feeling that she'd tell him her shoe size if he asked. After listening to her for a few minutes, he got to ask his questions.

He learned that she was a widow of long standing, childless, apart from having adopted an infant son. And two years later, a beautiful daughter from an orphanage. She'd named the boy William after her dead husband, who'd left her adequately provided for. The daughter, had already been named: Helen.

"You are a good listener," Mrs. Wells commented after he'd milked her dry of answers.

Yes, indeed. After waiting what seemed endlessly for approval, she'd adopted the beautiful Jamaican child and given her, and the boy she'd raised from an infant, the best she could afford. She loved them as though they had come from her.

She hadn't always approved of the company they kept, but not wanting to alienate them in any way, she'd hoped for the best and rolled with the punches until she could take it no longer.

When they got into drugs and did bad things to support their habit, Cynthia Wells had told them to shape up or ship out.

She hadn't seen hide-nor-hair of them since they'd left a little over six years ago. However, because of a baddy from Los Angeles named Basil Upton, they'd befriended, she suspected they'd gone there.

He thanked her for her time and hung up feeling like he'd won the jackpot at Vegas. He'd never known Helen's adopted surname, it hadn't been important to him and he'd never asked.

He made another cup of the instant coffee and sat in the kitchen ruminating, until he was sure he had it figured.

Helen Dekker, must have learned how to open the Bradley safe from William Wells.

She was an expert at archery, as was Charles. It fitted the puzzle perfectly.

He showered, dressed for the street, phoned Hickey at his apartment and told him that he'd established circumstantially at least, the culprit in the arrow murders and the shot at Steve.

"Let me guess, William Wells?"

"A possibility, James. You'll know after I confront the person with the evidence and make the arrest."

"You're making my headache worse, Carver."

"Have a good day, James; I'll talk to you later."

On hanging up on Hickey, he phoned Steve at the hospital and told him the news.

"Let me guess," Steve said, parroting Hickey, "the man in the moon?"

"You break me up," Carver countered.

"Well, what am I supposed to be in your eyes—a seer? From the few morsels you throw our way, not even Houdini would be able to figure it."

"Well, if you'll listen a while, I'll give you all the answers. Enough of them to make a charge of murder stick."

He didn't interrupt Carver while he unraveled the whole sordid mess. And he was truly sympathetic, knowing how difficult it would be for him to finger his friend Charles Dekker, for murder.

"I'll have Hickey make the arrest, Carver," Steve offered.

"I'll handle this myself, Steve. There won't be an easy way to break it to him. But after our years of friendship I owe him some consideration."

"That's only reasonable. When are you going to make all this happen?"

"Not until this evening. I hardly slept a wink last night and I'm going to head on back to bed after I present the district attorney with enough evidence to charge our friend Gino Padonti with attempted murder.

And this being Friday, Charles gets away from the restaurant early and cooks steaks at home on the barbi. I'll wait until they've finished dinner, about nine I'd guess, Charles doesn't like to eat early."

"Whatever you think, Carver. And for what it's worth, you, Hickey and Margo, have put this one to bed very close to your time frame. Have a good rest before your ordeal with Dekker and keep me posted. Thanks for the call, I'll talk with you later, champ."

After Padonti's arraignment, Carver headed to the Bel Air Sands to crash, but not before he'd turned off his phone.

He had dinner in their dining room, aware as he cut into his steak that even though it would be superlative, it wouldn't quite stack up to what Charles Dekker served.

It was an exceptionally warm evening with hardly the hint of a breeze. He drove with a heavy heart to the Dekker residence, and didn't bother to answer the cell phone that was interrupting his thoughts.

A half hour later he pulled to a stop under the portico. The front door was wide open, undoubtedly to stimulate a cross draft as Charles wasn't partial to air conditioning. Although his residence was equipped with it, he used it as a last resort.

As he was about to ring the chime, Helen came to the door wearing a concerned look. "Hello, Carver. What brings you at this hour?"

"Business, Helen. I've come to talk with Charles."

"Come in, then." She smiled and stood aside as he walked into the foyer of their beautiful home.

He saw Charles coming towards him, with hand extended in greeting.

Carver ignored the gesture, and walked towards the study, aware that Helen was trailing. Looking over his shoulder he said, "I'd like to talk to you in private, Charles."

When they entered the study and Charles closed the door, it didn't fully latch and remained slightly ajar. Carver wasn't concerned about that, and suspected that Helen would be listening in. At least this way, he wouldn't have to tell her to her face that her husband was a murderer, and she could deal with her emotions in the privacy of the hallway.

Charles sat nearby the unlit fireplace in his favorite chair, as Carver plunked himself onto a leather sofa alongside his friend. He could readily see that Charles was nervous, as though he already knew what Carver was about to disclose. So, looking unflinchingly at him, he started in.

"*It was you, who took that shot at me in my bathroom. Why, Charles?*"

Dekker lowered his head to avoid looking at him and remained silent.

"I'll tell you why," Carver continued, "you thought I was getting too close to solving the arrow murders. *You,* were the one who killed Bradley and Spencer. They were blackmailing you about Helen being a hooker before she married you, isn't that right?"

Charles lifted his head and looked at Carver, deeply concerned. He appeared ready to respond, but Carver didn't want to hear him, just yet.

"Morton Bradley, alias John Harvey, played on your sense of pride and your love for your wife. And knowing Helen, he guessed that she would pack up and leave you out of shame, once she learned that you knew of her sordid past. Isn't that right, Charles?"

"Yes," he answered very softly. "They were blackmailing me for years. They showed me photos that were disgusting. And knowing Helen's false pride, I had to keep it from her that I knew of her past. But I didn't kill either of them. The shot I took at you was only to try and scare you off the case. I figured if I came close enough to frighten you, you might throw in the towel on this one. But after firing the shot and seeing you drop out of sight, I was fearful that I really had killed you."

"You know me better than being a quitter who'd drop this or any other case. But you're not shoving the innocent bit down my craw. You worked the killings through William Wells; Helen's adopted brother. You learned from him, that he had a secret method of opening up the back of Bradley's safe from the outside wall off the balcony."

"No. That is simply not true."

"You know damn well it is. The Bradley mansion is on the other side of the small park in back of your place. You used one of your light aluminum ladders, got to the top of the wall and lowered it to the other side. Presto, he was fair game for your crossbow if his safe was open, and I guess it usually was. You climbed the lattice ladder beneath the ivy, opened the safe from the back, took out the negatives of the dirty pictures of Helen, found that Bradley was in your sights, and you shot him out of sheer hatred."

"That's not true, Carver."

"You're damn right it's true. You recruited her adopted brother William, to shoot Spencer, so you could clean out the partnership for good, but he got my friend Steve Holgate, instead. I don't know all the time sequences yet, but I will."

"William Wells and Helen, are adopted children to a Mrs. Cynthia Wells. They grew up as brother and sister in the small town of Wilmette, outside of Chicago. If I hadn't been so sloshed on Jamaican rum that night over here a little over four years ago, when Helen was showing her photo album, I would have solved this case in a couple of days. I felt strongly that I'd seen this fellow Wells before. His currently clean-shaven face, well groomed mustache and short hair, is what put me off from making the tie in to his hippy image in that group photo."

The study door opened wide on silent hinges. Helen Dekker stood in the doorway looking proud and haughty. In her hand she held a silver-plated revolver pointed at Carver's head, and her hand didn't waver even a fraction of an inch.

"It's not true, Carver," she said venomously. "Charles must have figured the angles, and took the shot at you to protect me. He probably hoped you'd be too busy with your other business to continue with the case."

"Put that gun away, Helen." Carver said sternly as the computer in his head spun out the real answers. "Good God, but I'm stupid." he mouthed forcefully, showing raised eyebrows and a distinct frown. "It just came to me. In those album pictures you were showing that night I was pleasantly sloshed on rum here, you were wearing a diamond and emerald brooch. And *that* is also what's been tugging at my memory all this time. I'll be damned."

"Yes, you're right," Helen admitted.

"Then Bradley and Spencer were blackmailing you, as well."

Figuring that she wouldn't pull the trigger on a friend, he got up from the couch to take the gun from her.

He was wrong. In the confined area of the study the roar of the silver plated.45 in her hand sounded like a rehearsal for a war.

He fell back onto the couch out of surprise and read the maniacal look in her eyes.

"The next shot won't be over your head," she threatened.

From the look of her, he knew that she meant it. Charles sat glued to his chair while his world was falling apart before his eyes, and he couldn't stop it.

"I didn't know those f—- king bastards were blackmailing Charles, too. Now that I do, I'm glad I killed them." Her eyes were glassy with rage and her choice of words reflected her past life.

"My brother William, told me how to open the safe. It happened like you said. I saw the light go on in his study while I was in the park and went back for the ladder. I took the pictures, the negatives, and a little box with what I thought was my brooch. I killed that rotten bastard, but I didn't discover that I'd taken the wrong brooch until about three in the morning, when I woke after taking a pill to make me sleep." She paused, licked her dry lips and continued. "My brother William and I, knew that Bradley and Spencer frequently watched the Tonight Show together. And that Spencer, having just returned from a holiday, would be there. William was to keep an eye out for Spencer, while camped out with a rifle in the small park. He told me the next day that he'd fallen into a deep sleep from the warmth of the night air and having smoked a couple of reefers. When he woke up and saw Spencer and two other men on the entrance landing, he put the scope on the guy he was sure was Spencer, shot him and took off like a rabbit down the hill in his car."

Having talked for a lengthy time while holding the gun aimed at Carver, Helen sighed noticeably. Her world was falling apart, but she hadn't let down her guard one iota. The revolver in her hand never wavered.

Carver sat glued to the couch while looking very concerned at the turn of events. That gun was still pointed at him. He would have to bide his time and hope for the best as Helen continued.

"As Charles was sound asleep in his bedroom," she continued, "I went back to exchange the brooch, saw the safe was empty and open in the study. And who should be sitting there looking like he'd lost his best friend—that son of a bitch, Victor Spencer. That was the point at which I became aware that the murder of Bradley was common knowledge, that the police had been there while I was sound asleep from the pills. I returned for my crossbow, went back and plugged the creep right through the heart. He was supposed to have been shot dead by my brother William, who mistook your friend Steve Holgate for Spencer, shot him and took off."

Carver shook his head over his shortcomings.

"What are you looking so perturbed about, lover boy? Did you think I was above murder?"

"It's doubtful if many of us are, Helen, if pushed far enough. I'm just annoyed with me, for not remembering that brooch of yours sooner. Charles was capable of paying the blackmail demanded, but you would have to resort to flogging your jewelry. I'm sorry, Helen. Sorry about the whole mess you've gotten into."

"I'm sorry too, Carver. You've been a good friend to both of us, up to now. I don't want to kill you—but now I have to."

Two ear-shattering shots rang out.

The one meant for Carver hit Charles in the shoulder. He'd anticipated his wife's timing and dove in front of his friend.

The other blast came from Margo's piece and got Helen through the heart. She dropped like a stone, dead before her body reached the bearskin rug at her feet.

Margo looked devastated, lowered the gun and raced over to Carver who'd gotten to his feet.

On being captured in his open arms and hugged close, she looked up at him and said, "It's a good thing your friend Steve Holgate finally recalled seeing that brooch of Helen's at a policeman's ball a few years back. He tried to reach you on your cell phone less than an hour ago, but you wouldn't answer. He wanted to tell you he thought the murderer was Helen Dekker, not Charles. So he phoned and told me to get over here real quick, and that I wasn't to hesitate using my gun if you were in danger."

Carver kept her hugged close, looked into the warmth of those deep brown eyes and they kissed passionately.

He smiled down at her, "Thank you for being here and for saving my life, partner."

She gave him a coquettish smile that instantly lit a fire in his heart. "Partner?"

"Yes, in more ways than one, Margo. Too much water has gone under the bridge since I last asked if I could bring you flowers."

"Will wonders never cease?" she remarked and smiled joyfully as they turned to walk hand-to-hand from the room.

§§§§§

Thank you for buying this detective mystery & love story. I sincerely hope you enjoyed it and will tell a friend.

Norm Wise

Printed in the United States
138396LV00001B/20/P

9 781606 934197